Lightning streaked the angry sky

The small plane battled through the storm. Visibility was zero but there was no real danger. The instruments were functioning, radio contact was clear. The pilot switched to the control tower and gave his position.

The air traffic controller's voice came back urgently: "88-Lima, say your altitude."

"Descending through nine hundred," the pilot responded calmly.

"Pull up!" screamed the voice in his earphones. "Pull up!"

The cloud cover suddenly broke and there, squarely in front of the speeding plane, loomed the tallest skyscraper in downtown Houston....

DRILLING *for* DEATH

John Wolfe

A RAVEN HOUSE MYSTERY FROM

W✦RLDWIDE

TORONTO · LONDON · NEW YORK

Raven House edition published September 1981

Second printing September 1981

ISBN 0-373-63007-7

Printed in Canada

1

I ALMOST TRIPPED over the bartender.

It wasn't his fault. He was just doing his job, threading his way across the room with a dozen drinks jiggling on the silver tray balanced on his arm. But the room he was crossing—that's what threw me. It looked like the kind of room Hugh Hefner would have dreamed up.

It wasn't a big room—maybe sixteen feet by twenty—furnished entirely in black and gold. The black leather bar along one side was spiked with brass buttons. A huge gold velvet couch, covered with black leopardlike spots, spread clear across the other end. And huddled between, thirty or forty of Houston's Beautiful People were having a party.

Looking straight across, between the bar and the couch, I could see a dozen rows of seats, and below—way below—the artificial turf of the Harris County Domed Stadium, otherwise known as the Astrodome. A football game was in progress, but nobody seemed to be paying any attention.

So this, I thought, is Jeppsen Oil Tool Company's private Sky Box.

A small blonde in a white V-neck dress came up and said, "Hi! You must be new here!"

Looking down from my six-foot-two height, I could almost see her navel, but I tried to concentrate on her round face and said, "Yeah, I'm Johnny McCoy. I'm supposed to meet Roger Lathrop. Is he here?"

"Sure, over there on the sofa. The little bald guy with the glasses. But how about having a drink with me first? I'm Laurie Jeppsen."

"Glad to know you. And thanks. Scotch on the rocks."

She called over her shoulder to the slim bartender: "Carlos, fix Mr. McCoy a Scotch on the rocks, please. And I'll have another Vodka martini while you're at it." She turned back. "Glad you joined the party. It's getting dull. But you look like something the Oilers could use down there on the field. Are you a football player?"

"Ex-football player," I said. "Very ex. No, I'm in the PR business. Going to be doing some work for the company."

"Oh, yes, I heard dad mention your name. From New York, right?"

"Originally Ohio. But that's right. I'm based in New York."

The bartender handed us our drinks. She clinked hers against mine. "Cheers! How long are you going to be in town?"

"I don't know. That depends. Probably a couple of weeks."

"How about letting me show you some of the sights? Houston's quite a swinging town."

Normally I don't mix business with pleasure, but Laurie's eyes held a promise that wasn't easy to resist. So I said, "Sure, I think I'd enjoy that.

But right now I'd better check in with Roger Lathrop.''

"Okay, let me introduce you." She took my hand—holding it tighter than necessary—and led me over to the sofa. "Roger, this is Johnny McCoy. Says he's looking for you." Having made the introduction, she edged away, saying, "Don't get lost, Johnny. I'll be around.''

Lathrop got up and held out a small hand. "Hello there, Johnny. Glad you made it. When did you get in?''

"About an hour ago.''

"Well, we've got a lot to talk about. Everybody thinks we're all getting rich in this business. Nobody realizes how tough it is to make a buck these days. Maybe you can help put the real story across.''

Looking around that room, it didn't seem to me that anybody was starving. Even the bartender's getup must have set somebody back a couple of hundred dollars. But I wasn't about to argue.

Lathrop smiled cordially. "Anyway, we can talk about that at the office tomorrow. Tonight, let's just get acquainted. Bart should be here soon. He's been out on a rig in the Gulf for the past two days. Still handles the tough jobs himself. The helicopter is bringing him right here to the Dome.''

"I'm looking forward to meeting him," I said. "He must be quite a guy.''

Lathrop's tone was almost reverent. "He *is* quite a guy. One of a kind. Drive? That man never stops. I just hope he'll relax a little when he gets here this evening. This is kind of a preconvention

party, you know. The company just turned
twenty-five. We've got reason to celebrate.''

I'd heard about that, of course. Who hadn't. In
twenty-five years, Bart Jeppsen had forged his
firm into a strong rival to Howard Hughes's old
outfit. Jeppsen Oil Tool Company was now one of
the dominant factors in the worldwide search for
more energy. Its drilling tools—called ''rock bits''
in the industry—were used by practically all the
major and minor oil producers and drilling
operators around the globe. Of the billions of
dollars that were invested every year in oil wells,
a healthy slug went into the coffers of Jeppsen
Tool. The only reason the company wasn't listed
on the Big Board was that Bart Jeppsen still
owned all the stock. Nobody knew how much he
was worth, but if he'd ever had a hankering for
New York City he could have bought it. Roger
Lathrop was executive vice-president. He handled
the financial and administrative end of the
business—and had ever since the beginning. But
big Bart was the driving force behind it all. To
most of the world, he *was* Jeppsen Oil Tool Company.

How did I get the account? My business card says
Johnny McCoy Associates, but the ''Associates''
consists only of Marsha Henley who does the typing and runs the room and a half on Third Avenue
we use as an office. I'm not, let's face it, J. Walter
Thompson. But I did snag one big account a few
months ago—Amalgamated Industries—and Ira
Harcourt, Amalgamated's Chairman of the Board,
had vast connections. So he'd recommended me to
Bart Jeppsen. It was that simple. After three years

in the PR business, I'd finally discovered that among the top echelons of corporate society, things usually *were* that simple.

I was about to make more small talk with Lathrop when the loud hubbub of conversation was sharply interrupted by a yell from Carlos, the bartender. Holding the telephone receiver in one hand, he called to Lathrop in a voice that was almost a scream. "Mr. Lathrop! Come here quick! It's from Grundy Aviation at Hobby. You'd better talk to 'em right away!"

Sensing the distress in Carlos's voice, Lathrop was already at the bar. Grabbing the phone from Carlos, he spoke crisply into the mouthpiece. "Hello, this is Roger Lathrop. What is it?"

There was a short pause. "He's *what*? Oh, no! God!" Lathrop's pink face turned the color of cigarette ashes. "When did it happen?" Another short pause. "How?" Then, "Oh, my God!"

A longer pause. "Yes, yes, of course. I'll want to go out there at once. Pick me up as quickly as you can. I'll be waiting at the pad downstairs. Thanks." Lathrop's hand was trembling as he put down the receiver.

Into the hollow silence of the room, Lathrop told us the shattering news. "The helicopter exploded. Right after takeoff from the rig. Bart's dead."

2

INSTANTLY THE GALA SKY BOX took on the atmosphere of a morgue. Everybody spoke at once, but only in hushed whispers. Hands stopped gesticulating. Smiles disappeared. Faces glazed over. To Bart Jeppsen's friends and associates, Lathrop's words struck like the announcement of a presidential assassination.

Lathrop rushed over to a regal-looking woman who looked ready to faint. He clasped her hands firmly. "Cynthia, I'm deeply sorry," he said shakily. "I don't know what else to say."

"Oh, God, Roger! I don't believe it." She shook her head helplessly. "You know Bart and I haven't been close these last few years. The company always meant more to him than I did. But this...." Her voice trailed off.

"I know, Cynthia. We all feel the same way. I'll get Laurie to drive you home." He turned to the cute blonde. "Laurie, take your mother right home, will you? Give her a tranquilizer...anything. Wait, maybe it'd be better to call Dr. Barnstone. He can give her a strong sedative. I'll be over in the morning."

A flabby young man in a yellow leisure suit spoke up shrilly. "What about me? Nobody ever worries about *me*! Don't you think I care, too?"

Lathrop's jaw muscles tightened. "Maybe that's your trouble, Randy. Maybe you've been worried about too damned much your whole life!" He caught himself. "Sorry. This is a hell of a shock to all of us. Why don't you go home with your mother and Laurie. There's nothing you can do to help here." He turned to the crowd. "Please, folks, let's just break up the party quietly. You'll all be kept informed."

The thirty or forty Beautiful People silently moved out. Minutes later, other than Carlos, the bartender, who was busily emptying ashtrays, the only people remaining were Lathrop, myself and a slender brunette I hadn't noticed before. She stood motionless at the bar, saying nothing, just waiting.

Lathrop looked at her. "Lisa! Are you still here?" He didn't really seem surprised.

"You know me, Roger. I'm always here. Somehow I think he still needs me—maybe even more now."

"Of course, Lisa. I know how you must feel." He turned to me and said, "Johnny, this is Lisa Wallace, Bart's personal secretary. You'll find out soon enough, so I might as well tell you: they've worked very closely together ever since Lisa joined the company right out of college."

I caught his drift but made no comment other than to say, "Hello, Lisa. I'm sure this is a blow to everyone."

Lathrop then seemed to gather himself together. "Look you two...Grundy Aviation is sending over a chopper to take me out to the rig. They usually don't fly at night—only in emergencies. But I'd say this *is* an emergency. Why don't you both come with me? I know how much it means to you, Lisa. . . and, Johnny, I suspect we're going to need *your* help now more than before.''

Ten minutes later, as Lathrop, Lisa Wallace and I stood waiting outside the shining round hulk of the Dome, Grundy Aviation's red and white Bell helicopter fluttered down, kicking tiny specks of dust off the pavement. The pilot, a freckle-faced redheaded kid, waved us aboard. Lisa and I climbed in back; Lathrop, sat up front next to the pilot. The whine of the rotor quickened as we lifted off the pad and headed south toward the Gulf.

To tell the truth, helicopters scare me. As an ex-Marine pilot in Viet Nam, I've logged over three thousand hours in airplanes—everything from trainers to jets—and I still get a kick, out of flying my own '58 Bonanza. I'd made it to Houston with only one stop in Atlanta, and the Bonanza was now parked outside the Grundy Aviation hangar at Hobby Airport. So, as I say, flying is old hat to me. Fun, yes. A concern, no.

But helicopters—they're something else. With no visible means of support, they always make me feel as if I'm riding a Ferris wheel that's gone on the blink. I just don't trust them.

But the pilot seemed to know his business. Twenty minutes after takeoff, the lights of Galvestor came into view, then disappeared as we headed out toward the black void that was the Gulf of Mexico.

Moments later, there was a brilliant streak of illumination. The vast expanse of water looked like a chocolate birthday cake with bright candles poking up everywhere, as oil rigs lit up the sky. Finally, steering between the candles, the helicopter came to the farthest rig and settled down inside the blue outline of lights around the octagonal pad. The pilot shut down the engine and we climbed out.

First to greet us was a lean man in tan overalls, whom Lathrop introduced as Charlie Delman, drilling superintendent of Calco Oil, the company that owned the rig. "Greetings!" he said trying to put up a front. "Normally I'd say welcome aboard, but I'm afraid this isn't anything normal. Jesus! I've been in the oil patch for over twenty years, but never in my life. . . ."

Lathrop was all back to business. "How did it happen?"

"It just happened, Roger, that's all. Bart got the bit working—he always does. . . or always did— and then got aboard the chopper with Herb Grundy. They took off, headed north, and just seconds later the whole goddamn sky lit up. I mean, it was like seeing the frigging world disintegrate! One big orange flame and a blast that almost knocked over the goddamn rig. Never saw anything like it. Hope I never do again. Jesus! I wish to hell we'd just let it go as another dry hole!"

"Don't blame yourself, Charlie. It couldn't have been an accident. Somebody must have planted a bomb on that chopper. And whoever had it in for Bart could have done it anywhere."

"Yeah, I guess, you're right. But it sure doesn't make me feel any better."

"Me either, Charlie. And Herb was the pilot. That's a damn shame, too. Has his wife been notified?"

The freckle-faced kid who'd flown us out to the rig spoke up at that point. "If you don't mind, I'd like to tell Martha myself. I'll drive over to the house soon as we get back. Those two have been like parents to me."

"Sure, that's okay," Lathrop said. "And I'll take care of calling the police. Bart's death will be the biggest case they've handled around here since the Joan Hill murder—probably bigger."

There didn't seem to be much else to say—and certainly nothing to do—so after a few more minutes of meaningless talk, we reboarded the helicopter and headed back to Houston.

We didn't try to talk above the whine of the rotor, but we were all thinking the same thing: Bart Jeppsen was clearly a man with thousands of friends, but also many enemies. It wouldn't be easy to find out who had killed him.

3

THE CYLINDRICAL MASS of the Astrodome was still bathed in white light, standing starkly against the sky, as we approached. But it was apparent that the ball game had ended. Thousands of twin headlight beams were snaking their way out of the parking lot and along the 610 Loop toward Houston's widespread suburbs. The young pilot eased us gently down onto the pad. He opened the door for our exit, said good-night and lifted the chopper back up into the cloudless night.

Lathrop said, "Johnny, do you have a car?"

"No, I'll rent one tomorrow. I came over here as soon as I could. Just dropped my suitcase off at the Shamrock and caught a cab."

Lisa spoke up. "That's all right, Roger. Why don't you go home. I'll be glad to drive him back to the hotel. Okay with you, Johnny?"

"Sure, that'd be fine. Thanks."

"All right, I'll say good-night," Lathrop said. "We'll all be thinking a lot clearer in the morning. Can you be at the office tomorrow at nine, Johnny?"

"Sure thing. I'll see you then. Again, Mr. Lathrop, I'm terribly sorry about what happened."

"We all are, Johnny. It's a miserable thing. Just awful. But I'm glad you're here. As I said, we're going to need your help more than ever now. I know Bart would have wanted us to carry on, and it's going to take a hell of a PR job to let the industry know we *can* carry on—without him." And with that, Lathrop stepped to his car and drove off into the night.

Lisa's car was on the other side of the lot, so we had a few minutes' walk. The air was still but cool, cooler than we were at that moment. Neither of us said much. Nor did we talk at all during the short drive to the Shamrock. Lisa seemed deep in thought—sad thought—and I didn't want to interrupt her reverie. But her grip on the wheel was firm, her movements controlled as she threaded her Grand Prix expertly through Houston's late-evening traffic.

Finally, as the green-topped roof of the Shamrock Hotel loomed into view and we turned into the curved driveway, she said, "How about buying me a nightcap, Johnny?"

"Fine with me. Sure you want to?"

"Yes, I'm okay now. But I could use a drink. And maybe it'd help to talk."

I pressed a dollar into the ready hand of the green-uniformed doorman, and we stepped into the Shamrock's opulent lobby. Once the only first-rate hotel in Houston, it was still one of the city's finest. Lisa led me through the twin doors to Trader Vic's, and we settled ourselves into the deep rattan chairs beside the lantern-lit bar. An Oriental girl in Hawaiian costume brought our drinks.

Then, as if a dam had burst, Lisa opened up. "I guess it's no secret that Bart and I had more than a business relationship. Everybody knew it, including Cynthia."

"Yes, I gathered that. He must have been some sort of guy."

"Sure was. To the company—and the whole world—he was an absolute tower of strength. Like a rock. But to me, he was the sweetest, gentlest man, I've ever known. I'll tell you, Johnny, under that steel skin of his, there was a heart. I mean a real heart." Lisa's voice was clear, but the ice in her glass made little tinkling sounds as she spoke.

We were both thinking about it, so I came out with it.

"Who do you think might have done it, Lisa?"

She gave a deep sigh. "I hate to say it, but there are a lot of people who didn't like Bart. Still, I can't imagine anyone hating him *that* much."

"Who stood to gain the most with him gone?"

"Well, of course, Cynthia will inherit millions. So will Randy and Laurie—and I guess you saw that Randy isn't exactly anybody's favorite. Bart always wanted him to be a real man like himself. He never was, never will be. So they certainly didn't get along."

"What does he do for a living?"

"Not much of anything. Just goofs off, mostly. Bart tried to cut off the handouts a dozen times, make him work like everybody else, but Cynthia's always taken pity on him. So she writes him a check whenever he runs short. Damned if I know why."

"How about Laurie?"

"She's still at Rice. Kind of a flaky kid, but other than that she seems okay."

"Do you happen to know how the two of them figure in Bart's will?"

"Yes, I was a witness when Bart signed it. They each come into a million-dollar trust fund. Of course, Cynthia gets the bulk of the estate."

"Anybody else with any kind of motive?"

"There's Roger. He truly worshiped Bart, but I suspect he also resented him. Let's face it, Bart was always the hero. Roger was only his second banana."

"What happens now?"

"That's easy. Roger takes over. They had an irrevocable buy-sell agreement, backed by a hefty insurance policy, to cover themselves in case anything ever happened to either one of them. I remember typing it up a few years ago."

"So that means several people had strong motives. None of them were out at that rig—they were all at the party—but any of them could have gotten somebody who *was* at the rig to plant that bomb. I'm sure the cops will want to question the whole crew."

Lisa laid her hand on mine. "Will *you* talk to them yourself?"

"Me! Why me?"

"Your time's being well paid for, isn't it?"

"Sure! But I've been hired to do a PR job, not to get mixed up in a murder. Look, I know Bart and you were. . . well, good friends. I'm sorry as hell it happened. Really. But I never even met the guy!"

For the first time, her voice began to crack. "Johnny, I can't expect you to feel the same way I do about it. Bart was the biggest thing that ever happened to me. To you, he was just a passing client. I realize that. But from your questions a couple of minutes ago, I thought you might be concerned, too.''

"Concerned, yes, but. . .''

"And this isn't the first homicide case you've been involved with,'' she pressed on. "Bart told me about the Chip Lloyd murder you solved in New York recently. Even with the Mafia after you.''

"Sure, but. . .''

"And, as I understand it, Chip Lloyd was really only a small-time comic, right?''

"I guess you could say that. He was killed during his act at the Bar None, Jill Harcourt's place. Jill's father, Ira Harcourt, was the president of Amalgamated Industries. He was my client. And, yes, Jill had got herself mixed up with some pretty rough characters. But what's all that got to do with anything?''

"Two things. For one, Jeppsen Oil Tool is your client, too. That hasn't changed. And if I know Roger Lathrop, it won't be a cut-rate assignment, either. You can write your own ticket. Second, you admit that Chip Lloyd was small-time. Well, Bart Jeppsen was big-time. I mean, *really* big-time. And not just to me. To the whole world.'' She took another sip of her drink, then looked up at me intently. "Johnny, do you fully realize how a company like Jeppsen Oil Tool fits into the whole scheme of things—what it means to our entire economy?''

"Not really. I just got here, remember?''

"Well, let me fill you in a little. Roger will un-
doubtedly tell you more tomorrow, but now that
you're on the payroll, this is as good a time as any
to start briefing you on the broad scope of it."

Under ordinary circumstances, I'd have found
Lisa's obvious total involvement with her job as
well as her boss somewhat amusing. I might have
grinned and said, "Okay, Teach, educate me!"
But, clearly, these were not ordinary circumstances. So I remained silent as she went on.

"See, Johnny, all the public ever hears about
these days is the profit made by the companies like
Exxon, Shell, Texaco, Calco Oil and the rest of the
big giants, And with the price we all have to pay
for our gas, I guess that's understandable. But
what so few people ever think about is the *cost* of
producing oil—and the risk. It's like no other
business in the world. For instance, take your own
PR agency. When you first set up shop, you didn't
know exactly how much business you'd do or how
much money you'd take in, right?"

Thinking back to the day I quit Fullerton-Davis
Advertising and got Marsha Henley to take a flyer
with me on Johnny McCoy Associates—against the
advice of just about everybody—I had to smile at
that. But all I said was, "I sure as hell didn't.
Nobody does in any business."

"Exactly," Lisa agreed. "But here's the point.
You *did* know you'd do *some* business. Maybe not
enough, but some. But when an outfit like Calco
Oil drills a hole in the ground, like the one we saw
tonight, they invest millions without knowing
whether they'll get back a dime!"

"Sounds like shooting craps," I observed.

"You got it, Johnny. That's exactly what it is—with a lot bigger chips than you'll find in Vegas. And that's why companies like Jeppsen Oil Tool are so terribly important. It's folks like us who help make it all pay off—for Calco Oil and everybody else."

"Because you supply the equipment to do the job."

"Yes, we supply the equipment." She cocked her head to one side. "But it's more than that. We also provide the talent. What really counts is the genius of men like Bart Jeppsen—and I don't use the word lightly. That's why Bart himself was out at the rig tonight. You heard Charlie Delman say it yourself. Jeppsen Oil Tool didn't get that bit working; *Bart* did."

"So that's what Roger had in mind when he said my help would be needed now more than before."

"Precisely. It won't be easy to sell the idea that the company is worth a damn without Bart. But that's the least we can do for him—make sure that Jeppsen Oil Tool *does* go on. And the longer Bart's murder remains unsolved, the tougher it's going to be for all of us."

She almost had me sold. "I'm beginning to see what you mean."

"There's one more thing I need to tell you, Johnny." The ice in Lisa's drink tinkled more loudly. She put down the glass and clenched her fists. For the first time her eyes began to moisten. "I told you that Bart and I had a very special kind of relationship."

I could see that she had something bottled up inside that was struggling to get out, so I just nodded silently.

"Well, that's what I meant. We *had* a special relationship. Past tense."

"You don't mean that Bart . . . ."

She shook her head quickly. "Oh, no. No. With Bart it was still in the present. What I mean is that *I* was about to drop him." Now that she'd started to let it all hang out, her words came pouring like a torrent. "For years now, Bart's been my whole life. There was nothing he didn't do for me—I mean nothing—except for one thing. And that's the one thing he couldn't do."

"You mean marry you," I said softly.

"That's right. Oh, for the first couple of years it wasn't important. We both enjoyed what we had together. But then, especially lately, I began to think about the future. I'm not getting any younger, Johnny. And just last week I finally made up my mind to break it off." She began to sob softly. "Would you believe that I was going to tell him tonight. I really was. Now I'll never need to tell him!"

"Maybe it's better this way," I said, still softly.

"Perhaps you're right, Johnny." She straightened her shoulders. "But don't you see? That's still another reason why you've *got* to help find out who killed him. For my sake, as well as his. *Please*."

I could see that Bart Jeppsen had had himself quite a girl. She'd sure worked a PR job on me. "Okay, Lisa," I said. "I'll do what I can."

Her hand, again resting on mine, gave a squeeze.

"Thanks, Johnny, I hoped we could count on you."

We finished our drinks, and I walked her outside. We shook hands and said good-night. She gave me a soft peck on the cheek, got in her Grand Prix and drove off.

Riding up to my room in the Shamrock Hotel elevator, I had only one thought: whoever killed Bart Jeppsen wouldn't appreciate my interference in the case. He just might start gunning for me.

Here we go again.

4

AT 8:55 THE NEXT MORNING, Lisa Wallace ushered me into Roger Lathrop's office at Jeppsen Tool. I could see immediately that I wasn't his first visitor of the day.

Lathrop rose from behind his walnut desk and said, "Thanks for getting here so promptly, Johnny." He shook my hand and motioned to a stocky man seated in one of the two armchairs facing the desk. "This is Lieutenant Mendez of the Houston Police Department. He's going to be in charge of the case. And, Lieutenant," he went on, "this is Johnny McCoy from New York who's handling some public relations for us."

Mendez had a well-manicured, pencil-thin mustache that somehow didn't go with his round face. We shook hands and mumbled the usual greeting.

Lathrop apparently had finished telling Mendez the few facts known at the time, for the plainclothes cop was just closing his notebook. "The first step," he said, fingering his mustache to make sure it was still there, "is to visit that rig and question everyone who was there last evening. Can you arrange for me to fly out right away?"

"Of course," Lathrop answered. "Johnny and I'll go with you." He pressed a button on the intercom behind his desk. "Lisa, call Grundy Aviation and tell them to have a chopper ready in twenty minutes, will you please? We'll be flying out to the rig immediately."

"Right," came Lisa's voice through the speaker.

Moments later, as Lathrop, Mendez and I stepped through the outer office, Lisa was hanging up the phone. "All set," she said. "They'll be waiting for you." She caught my eye as we were leaving and silently mouthed the words, "Thanks, Johnny."

Walking through the downstairs foyer of the building, I glanced up at the large, oak-framed photo that dominated the far wall. Bart Jeppsen's square-jawed face looked out at us confidently.

TWENTY MINUTES LATER we arrived at Hobby. Lathrop parked his blue Buick sedan in front of the corrugated steel hangar that said Grundy Aviation, and we entered the sparsely furnished lounge at the side. The motherly looking woman who had greeted me the previous evening was absent. A young girl in jeans and sweater was apparently filling in at the counter. Her eyes were red.

"Hello there, Mr. Lathrop," she said. "Mom stayed home today. Best thing for her, under the circumstances. God, what an awful thing! Dad went through two wars without a scratch—and now this! I know he wasn't as important as Mr. Jeppsen, but...." The red eyes welled up.

"I know, Mary," Lathrop said gently. "Your dad was a fine man. We'll all miss him."

The girl composed herself and said, "Jack is just checking out the chopper. Should be ready in a minute."

Just then, the freckle-faced helicopter pilot entered the lounge, his red hair tousled from the wind outside. "All set," he announced. "You folks ready to go?"

"Yes, indeed," Lathrop said.

"The sooner, the better," echoed Lieutenant Mendez.

Again, Lathrop sat up front next to the pilot; Mendez and I climbed in back. And, once again, the red-and-white Bell helicopter was flown expertly to the Calco Oil rig eighty miles out in the Gulf of Mexico.

Once more, we were greeted by the superintendent in charge of the operation, Charlie Delman. His leathery face looked pale and drawn; it was obvious he hadn't slept much the previous night. Lathrop introduced him to the police lieutenant and the investigation began.

"I understand that the helicopter exploded right after takeoff," Mendez began. "You saw it happen, did you?"

"God, yes, I saw it!" Delman answered. "The whole damn Gulf did!"

"Were you with Mr. Jeppsen when he got aboard?"

"Of course! Bart and I've known each other for years. I remember when he first started the company—I was fresh out of engineering school then. So I was the last to say thanks and good-night to him after he got the bit working. I was probably the last person to talk to him at all. Jesus!''

"Sorry I've got to ask these questions, Mr. Delman," the lieutenant went on. "Just how long was the helicopter here at the rig last evening?''

"Only a few minutes—maybe ten or fifteen. We didn't call for it to come out till we knew things were operating right.''

"How many men do you have working on the rig?''

"Well, the crews are rotated every few weeks. Figuring the tool pusher, rig hands, service reps and all the rest, we keep about a dozen men on hand all the time. That's about how many were here last night.''

"Are they still here?''

"Yes.''

"I'll want to talk to each of them individually, then. But first, let me ask you this...would it have been possible for any of them to get near the helicopter while it was parked on the pad?''

"Sure, I guess so. Most of them could have.''

"Did you happen to see anyone place anything aboard the helicopter—anything that might have contained a bomb?''

"No. But, then, I wasn't topside the whole time. Fact is, knowing it was Jeppsen Tool's twenty-fifth anniversary, Bart and I shared a drink together before he left.''

"Where was the pilot, Herb Grundy, all this time?''

"Well, I know he went to the head for a minute.

Then he probably chewed the fat with a couple of the guys."

"So someone could have gotten to that helicopter without being seen?"

"I guess so—someone must have. And I hope to hell you find out who it was."

"So do I, Mr. Delman," said the lieutenant grimly. "So do I."

Lathrop and I stood around for almost an hour while Mendez questioned each of the men on the rig. They were of varying ages, sizes and shapes, but they all had one thing in common—a tough, hard-bitten look around the eyes and mouth. I was learning fast that an oil rig was no place for weaklings.

I was also learning that the case wouldn't be easy to solve: none of the men had any information—or volunteered any—that would help pinpoint who was behind it all.

Then, just before we left, Charlie Delman came up with the obvious answer—the answer to one question, anyway.

"If no one else loaded that bomb on the chopper, Bart must have carried it aboard himself," he said. Lathrop, Mendez and I looked at him in amazement. "I mean without knowing it, of course," Delman went on. "See, he was taking a used-up bit back out with him. Wanted to check it in the lab. It was packed in a wooden carrying case. Could be the bomb was packed in with it!"

Mendez snapped his fingers. "That's it!" he said, fingering his mustache again. It was the first time he'd exhibited any form of excitement. "That's got to be it! Anybody could have slipped a bomb into a box like that, and no one would see it or even suspect its presence. But who put it there— and who paid him to? And why?''

Returning to Hobby in the helicopter, we were all thinking the same thing.

We were right back where we started.

5

IT WAS ALMOST ONE-THIRTY by the time we got back to Hobby, so Lathrop suggested having lunch before returning to the Jeppsen plant. Mendez and I both readily agreed.

Lathrop headed the Buick north along the Gulf Freeway, toward Houston. As the gleaming skyline came into view, the tall geometric shapes of the buildings and the elevated freeways crisscrossing in all directions reminded me of the covers of old *Popular Mechanics* magazines—the ones captioned "City of the Future."

But our conversation still revolved around the mystery of Bart Jeppsen's murder. Mostly, we were just talking in circles.

Lathrop exited the freeway just before reaching the center of the city and drove a few blocks before parking next to a massive, yet graceful white structure. "This is the Exxon Building," he told me. "Used to be the tallest in town, till Shell put up theirs."

We stepped inside the large lobby and climbed aboard the elevator that said "Petroleum Club Only." In moments we were whisked to the forty-third floor, where the elevator door opened out to a richly carpeted foyer with full-length glass windows surveying the city on all sides. Once again, I saw that if Houston is not exactly the land of milk and honey, it is indeed the land of oil and money.

At the entrance to the smartly appointed dining room, the maître d' greeted Lathrop with due respect and proper condolences, then led us to a corner table.

As the waiter left with our orders, Mendez repeated for the tenth time: "With no real clues to go on, this is going to be an extremely difficult case to solve. I appreciate your help, Mr. Lathrop."

"Of course. Anything I can do. Anything, just ask."

"Well," said Mendez, "Is there anything else you can tell me about Mr. Jeppsen's personal life? For instance, his marriage. Was it a happy one?"

"Happy as most these days, I guess. Bart and Cynthia met when he first started in the oil patch. He looked like a leader, even then."

"Did he have money then, too?"

"No, not really. Originally, the money was Cynthia's. She's the daughter of Haynes Randall, the senior partner of Randall, Quirt, Devereaux and Livesay." Then, to me, he added, "They're the biggest law firm in the southwest."

"She's still an attractive woman," I observed. "Must have been quite a catch."

"I guess you can say that," Lathrop answered. "But Bart never had any trouble finding female companionship, that's for sure. He pretty much had his pick. And, let's face it—you'll find this out anyway, Lieutenant—even after he and Cynthia were married, he always had a few other women

on the side. That is, until four years ago when Lisa
Wallace joined the firm. Since, then, he's only had
one. That girl was truly in love with the guy. She
knew there was no future in it—as far as marriage
goes, I mean. Bart never tried to con her about
that part of it. But, well. . . I guess that's the way
it happens sometimes.''

All that, of course, gibed with what Lisa had told
me the evening before at Trader Vic's. It also
meant that she hadn't revealed to Lathrop, or
probably anyone else, that she was about to drop
Bart—that despite her deep affection for the man,
the love affair was over. I naturally decided to
maintain the confidence.

Mendez then asked the obvious questions con-
cerning a possible motive—the same questions I
had asked Lisa—and Lathrop provided exactly the
same answers. Between mouthfuls of food, the
lieutenant kept making notes in his little black
book.

Finally, the waiter brought the check, which
Lathrop signed with a floruish, and we left. Walking out to the foyer, and riding down in the
elevator, we were again greeted by words of condolence and support on all sides. Lathrop obviously couldn't claim Bart Jeppsen's charisma, but he
did have friends.

Little more was said during the drive back to the
Jeppsen plant. As Lathrop nosed the Buick
through the gates, Mendez said, ''You can let me
out here, Mr. Lathrop. My car's parked right over
there. Thanks for the lunch—and for your help. I'll
be in touch.''

He was about to leave when I thought I'd better

say something about my own apparent involvement. "I'll be in touch with you, too, Lieutenant. That is, if you don't mind."

Mendez's dark eyes narrowed. "And why is that, Mr. McCoy? I thought your function was public relations. I'm afraid the Police Department can't help you much with that."

"It was," I said. "And it is. But I'm going to be doing a little looking into Bart Jeppsen's murder, too."

"Why? I'm sure you know your business, but we know ours. And that kind of help we don't need."

I shrugged helplessly. "I've been asked, that's all I can tell you."

"This is a free country, Mr. McCoy. And a big one. That's why my parents moved here from Tampico. But just stay out of my way. I've got a job to do—without interference, from you or anyone else." And with that he walked away. Under the circumstances, I couldn't really blame him.

Back in Lathrop's office, I got the obvious from him. "What was that all about, Johnny? We need Mendez's help and we need it badly. Just as we need yours. But let's not rock the boat—not any more than it's rocked already."

So I told Lathrop about my conversation with Lisa the night before—most of it, that is. I hadn't meant to hold out on him, but this was my first opportunity.

"Look," he said, "I know how Lisa feels—I feel the same way—and I guess in a way she's right. But I can see the lieutenant's point, too. So go ahead and check around if you must. I won't ask for a time sheet. But as Mendez said—and he made it pretty plain—just don't step on his toes. Fair enough?''

"Fair enough," I agreed.

"Fine! Let's go to work." He looked at his watch. "We've still got over an hour before closing—our hours are eight to five, you know. I gave you a break this morning. So why don't we set you up in Dave Marshall's office—he's our international sales manager and he'll be in Europe all month—and you can get started by studying up on the company." He pressed the intercom buzzer. "Johnny will be using Dave's office, Lisa. Fix him up with the usual stuff, will you? You know, catalogs, company history, product brochures, trade publications and so on."

Lisa's response came back immediately. "Will do, Roger."

Five minutes later, I was seated in a smaller office down the hall, and I spent the next hour poring over the mass of Jeppsen literature that Lisa had deposited on the desk in front of me.

It told the fascinating story of oil-well operations around the globe, the intricate combination of engineering science and human muscle that brings energy from the ground and powers the world. And I *was* intrigued. As Lisa had told me the previous evening, I was becoming involved in a totally unique business.

I began to see, too, how it all tied together to make Houston the fastest-growing major city in the country. An article in *Houston Magazine*, the monthly publication of the Chamber of Commerce, spelled it out in graphic terms.

"Over 1500 people a week move to our fair

city,'' the article pointed out. "Within a decade,
our population will exceed that of Dallas and Fort
Worth combined, and our metropolitan area will
rank seventh in the nation. And while Houston's
commercial base constantly expands ever wider,
the petroleum industry remains at the core of our
fantastic growth.''

Then it went on to explain further the relationship *within* the industry that Lisa had also
touched on. "Oil is to Houston what automobiles
are to Detroit. There are only a very few large
automakers in Detroit, but thousands of other
firms selling a multitude of various products and
services *to* the car manufacturers. The same business pattern applies here. The number of major oil
companies is relatively small, but those few
giants—and the smaller operators, too—all rely on
the thousands of firms that supply them with the
goods and services they need in the production of
petroleum. Without Dresser, Hughes, Halliburton,
Baker, Cameron, Jeppsen, Schlumberger and all
the rest, the oil wells of the world would dry up instantly. And so would Houston.''

Of course, several of these names were unfamiliar to me—they're not exactly household words
like Kodak and Coca-Cola—but I was able to deci-
pher at lest a partial explanation from some of the
ads in the trade magazines like *Oil and Gas Journal*.

I learned, for example, that Schlumberger mainly provides "logging" services—electronic surveys
printed out like a heart patient's electrocar-
diogram—to help pinpoint where the oil, if any,
is located. Cameron manufactures "Christmas

trees," the odd-shaped valve assemblies used to "complete" the top of the well. A few of the other companies, like Dressen, Halliburton and Baker International, offer diverse products and services through a multitude of divisions. Hughes, of course, is the company that was inherited by Howard Hughes when he was still a gangling juvenile. It was the giant that Bart Jeppsen took on when he founded Jeppsen Oil Tool. And, as one of the Jeppsen ads proclaimed: "Our rock bits drill the hole . . . deeper . . . cheaper."

As I say, I was fascinated. That, after all, is one of the kicks I get out of my business. I get to learn a little about a lot.

But my mind kept coming back to the question that was to haunt me—in every sense of the word—over the days ahead: who had murdered Bart Jeppsen?

And at the same time, I couldn't help wondering why Roger Lathrop was reluctant to have me delve into the case. As he'd said, Mendez had a point. There's such a thing as professional jealousy, among policemen as well as PR hucksters. I'd learned that in the past.

Besides, of course, Lathrop *was* paying me good money—damn good money—for my services. As the client, he had every right to dictate how I'd spend my time.

But, still, the question remained: didn't Lathrop *want* Bart Jeppsen's murder solved?

At that point, I had no idea what I'd be going through to find out.

6

THAT EVENING, I had a quick dinner alone in the Terrace Dining Room at the Shamrock. Then I holed up in my room for a couple of hours to draw up some initial promotional plans for Jeppsen Tool.

When I got in the next morning, Lisa gave top priority to typing them up for me, and by nine o'clock, I was back in Roger Lathrop's office. Seeing the work I'd done, he seemed a lot more cordial than he'd sounded the previous afternoon.

He read the four-page report quickly, put down his coffee cup and smiled appreciatively. "That looks good, Johnny, mighty good. You seem to have gotten a handle on this thing in a hurry."

"Yes, sir. I thought we'd better get moving on it as soon as possible. The longer we wait, the tougher it's going to be."

"Right! Good thinking. But please cut out the 'sir.' In the oil patch, everyone's on a first-name basis."

"Fine with me, Roger. Thanks. Anyway, as you can see, I think we ought to schedule a news conference for two o'clock this afternoon.

We can pass out that press release at the same time." I handed him another sheaf of bond paper. "Here's what I recommend for your opening statement."

Lathrop glanced at it briefly, nodded his approval and immediately called Lisa into the office. "Let's go ahead with this news conference for two o'clock," he told her. "Call all the radio and TV stations, the *Post* and the *Chronicle*, of course, and the major networks and wire services, too. Oh, and don't forget *The Wall Street Journal*."

Lisa's pencil flew over her steno pad as Lathrop spoke. She closed the cover and said, "Sure thing. Right away." Then she turned a smile in my direction and walked back to her desk in the next office.

Lathrop and I spent most of the rest of the morning discussing the other ideas in my proposal; a sales meeting to be held a week later, and a new ad campaign to begin as soon as possible.

"It's going to be difficult to pull our men out of the field again on such short notice," he commented. "Most of 'em were just here for the party, you know, but then I sent 'em all back to their regions."

"I'm aware of that," I said. "But I think it's necessary, especially with the regional and district managers. Otherwise we may lose them." I'd learned a long time ago that clients like to hear the word "we" instead of "you."

"Okay, I see your point. There's plenty of pirating in this business, and as the leader, we get hurt by it more than most. Yes, I guess it would be better to bring those guys in for a couple of days than leave them out there wondering what the hell is going on.''

I nodded. ''Exactly. I'll work with Lisa in setting up the arrangements.''

Then Lathrop raised a question about my advertising suggestions. ''This is quite a departure from what we've been doing,'' he pointed out.

''That's exactly why I think it might be a good idea,'' I said. ''The ads you've been running in the past are fine. But they all emphasize Jeppsen *products*. Right now I think we need to sell the Jeppsen *company*.''

''Yes, I guess that makes sense.''

And so it went. I could see that Lathrop had many of the traits of a good executive, including the willingness to accept advice from others.

Lisa had reserved a meeting room at the Petroleum Club for the news conference, and Roger proposed that we have lunch there first. I accepted, of course, but suggested that we take separate cars. He looked at me oddly, but agreed without comment. So Roger drove over in his Buick sedan, and I followed in my rented Cutlass.

Once again, we rode up to the forty-third floor in the ''Petroleum Club Only'' elevator, dined leisurely in the grill and then moved into the special meeting room off the lounge area.

The room was already a beehive of activity. A couple of dozen men and women, mostly young, mostly casually dressed, were busily setting up mikes, tape recorders, TV cameras and other communications hardware, while others waited patiently in chairs with notebooks on their laps. Off to the side, alone, sat Lieutenant Mendez. The grapevine obviously extended to the Houston Police Department.

At exactly 2:00 P.M., bright lights flooded the front of the room, and Lathrop stepped briskly to the podium, carrying the speech I had prepared for him.

"Ladies and gentlemen," he began, "you all know the tragedy that has struck our company and this great city and the entire world. And you already know as many of the details of Bart Jeppsen's murder as we do. We're all praying, as I know you are, that this dastardly crime will be solved and Bart's killer brought to justice as soon as possible. So our purpose in inviting you here today is not to discuss those tragic events. Rather, it is to tell you our plans—great plans, as Bart would have wanted—for the future."

The speech continued in that vein for another twenty minutes, after which Roger opened the floor for questions. It seemed to me that he fielded them pretty well. Perhaps he was getting used to the idea that now he was no longer second-in-command of the Jeppsen empire, that he could indeed, in his own way, fill Bart's shoes. And maybe, just maybe, he was even beginning to enjoy his new role of top banana. They say it happened that way with Harry Truman after the death of Franklin Roosevelt.

Finally a few minutes before three o'clock, the news conference ended, the copies of the press release were handed out and the meeting broke up.

Lathrop turned to me, obviously satisfied with his performance. "How do you think it went, Johnny?"

"Just fine, Roger," I said. "Really, I think you did a super job."

"Thanks. Couldn't have done it without that great speech you wrote for me. It seemed to hit exactly the right note."

"Look," I said. "Do you think you'll need me for the rest of the day?"

"No, I guess not. You've put in a damn good day's work already," Lathrop seemed to sense what I had in mind. He obviously must have known why I'd suggested taking two cars.

"Well, if it's okay with you, then, I've got some business to take care of."

At that moment, Lieutenant Mendez, who had listened intently, but quietly, throughout the news conference, sidled up just in time to overhear my last remark.

"That was a fine performance, Mr. Lathrop," he said, fingering his mustache. "And I presume that you, Mr. McCoy, had a hand in preparing the speech. As I suggested yesterday, I just hope you continue your pursuit of that kind of activity— *only* that kind of activity."

"Look, Mendez," I said. "Mr. Lathrop just gave me the rest of the day off. And what I do on my own time is my own business, not yours or anyone else's."

"Ah, but what you do here in Houston *is* my business, Mr. McCoy—that is, if it in any way impinges on our police work. You see, we have a saying for that in Spanish. Translated, it means: every farmer should plow his field, but stay out of his neighbor's.''

"And we have a saying in English, too," I shot back. "Translated, it means: get the hell off my back.''

This time I walked out on him.

7

FOLLOWING THE DIRECTIONS Lisa had given me, I headed the rented Cutlass out Allen Parkway and onto Kirby Drive, which led into the city's most exclusive residential area, River Oaks. In places, high brick walls hid the estates beyond; at times, the immense Colonial mansions of Houston's "oil rich" were exposed to view. Several of the wide lawns were being worked on by dark-skinned gardeners, and uniformed maids occasionally appeared wheeling children in baby carriages. Presumably, these palaces also had owners, but if so they remained invisible.

Coming to Inwood Drive, I turned into the driveway of Bart and Cynthia Jeppsen's stately home. With tall pillars guarding the broad white facade, it looked like something out of *Gone With the Wind*. I half expected Scarlett O'Hara to come giggling out the front door twirling a parasol. Instead, there was total silence. Then, as I parked in the circular drive and turned off the engine, I heard the sound of splashing water. Looking past the tennis court at the side of the house, I saw that the splashing was coming from an Olympic-size swimming pool in the back of the three-acre property. I walked past the ornate gazebo, rounded the tiled barbecue pit and approached the pool.

It was occupied by just one person, who was gaily romping in the shimmering blue water—Laurie Jeppsen. She swam the length of the pool, and then sensing my presence, stood facing me at the shallow end near the steps. Her tanned body was barely covered by a tiny red bikini.

"Hi!" she said. "If it isn't the very ex-football player."

"Hi yourself," I said. "Is your mother home?"

"No," she answered happily. "No one's home. Come on in."

"I *am* in," I said.

"No, silly, I mean in the pool."

"Sorry. I don't have a swimsuit."

Laurie shrugged and said, "Just a minute." She dived down briefly, made a couple of swift movements under water and came up holding two wisps of red cloth. She smiled at me. In fact, standing there in three feet of water, *all* of her smiled at me. "There," she said. "Now we're even."

I was just debating how to handle this situation—and thinking that Houston was indeed a friendly town—when I heard a car pull into the driveway. "Oh-oh," Laurie said. "I guess I'll have to catch you later. Mommy's home."

And indeed she was. As Laurie hurriedly refastened her bikini, Cynthia Jeppsen strode out on the patio. "Oh, Mr. McCoy," she said. "How nice of you to stop by. Can I fix you a drink?"

"No, thanks," I answered. "But I would like to talk with you for a minute if I can. I know this is a difficult time for you, but...."

"Certainly," she said. "Why not? I've already

done just about all the crying I can.'' She stepped to the bar at the side of the patio, mixed herself a gin and tonic and sat down on a wrought-iron chaise. "There, have a seat." She motioned me to a padded sofa. "What would you like to talk about?"

"Mainly about your husband, Mrs. Jeppsen. From everything I've heard, he was a marvelous man."

"You've heard right, Mr. McCoy. They just don't make them like that anymore. Jeppsen Oil Tool will go on, I know. Roger will see to that. But neither he nor anyone else can ever take Bart's place." For the first time, her voice began to crack a little.

"Mrs. Jeppsen," I said gently. "You're talking about Bart's place in the company. This isn't easy, but. . . well how about his place with you?"

"Oh, that!" She laughed a bit shrilly. "I guess it's no secret that Bart's place *was* the company. That's something I was never really part of."

"Yet the two of you remained married all these years," I pointed out.

"Sure we did—on paper. But *only* on paper." Then she turned and her eyes bored into me. "What's all this to you, Mr. McCoy?"

"Look, Mrs. Jeppsen," I said. "My job is PR, you know that. And, I hope I can be of some help to the company. But I've also been asked to lend a hand in the murder investigation. These questions have to come up."

"And who sicced you onto *that* little exercise? Lisa Wallace, I'll bet. If you want to know what happened to our marriage—especially the last few years—why don't you ask her?"

"I guess I already know the answer to that one, Mrs. Jeppsen. But in view of the situation between you and Bart—and between Lisa and Bart, too, for that matter—I'd say that you probably had as much reason to kill him as anyone. Sorry, but that's the way it's got to look."

Cynthia Jeppsen stood up abruptly. "That will be quite enough, Mr. McCoy." Now her voice was really shaking. "Here I've been going through holy hell—couldn't even give the man a decent funeral—and you come by with more of these goddamn questions. So I'll give it to you one time, and I'll give it to you straight: Bart and I had a lousy marriage. But that was his fault. Not mine. God knows I tried!"

"I'm sure you did, Mrs. Jeppsen," I said softly.

"Wait a minute! I'm not through! You asked me, and I'm going to tell you." She was almost shouting now. "Bart wasn't married to me; he was married to Jeppsen Oil Tool. But I wasn't about to give either of them up. Sure I had reason to kill him—plenty of reason—*but I didn't do it*. Now, Mr. McCoy, just get the hell out of here!"

Indeed, it seemed time for me to leave.

I was just getting into my car when I heard a voice much softer and friendlier than Mrs. Jeppsen's. Laurie was outside the front door, wearing a sleek green pantsuit. "Hello again," she said. "How about taking me out for dinner?"

Why not? "Sure," I said. "Climb in."

"Great! I know a cozy place where we can talk. And they also serve good stiff drinks."

That sounded like the best idea I'd heard lately.

8

LAURIE DIRECTED ME through a series of winding tree-lined streets, all with similarly imposing homes on both sides.

"Wow! Some neighborhood you live in," I commented.

She laughed. "Yeah."

"But it doesn't impress you, I guess."

"Not really. I don't think there's much difference between rich people and poor people."

Remembering F. Scott Fitzgerald's line, I added, "Except that they've got more money."

Then she got serious for a moment. "How about you, Johnny? Were you poor as a kid?"

"No, not poor. My dad ran a drugstore in Dayton. Still does. So we never really scrimped. But I've never lived like this."

"Maybe that's my trouble. I always have. But, hey, let's not get morbid about it." She laughed again. "We have a saying in River Oaks: 'If you've got it, don't flaunt it. Just enjoy it.' That's what we try to do."

"And I can see you succeed."

"Why not? That's what money's for, isn't it? Hell, come up with enough money and you can buy any place in River Oaks . . . well, almost any."

"What do you mean by almost?"

She laughed once more. "Well, there's one
story—it's supposed to be true—about a woman
who came here looking for a house. Her husband
had told her not to worry about the price.
'Just find the one you want,' he'd said, 'and I'll
buy it for you.' So she finally made her choice,
told him it was nice and big and had everything
she wanted, even a golf course. But he didn't buy
it."

"Why not?"

"It turned out to be the River Oaks Country
Club!"

That one got me laughing, too. Laurie had shown
a serious side of her makeup that I hadn't expected. But she *was* fun to be with.

Finally, still following Laurie's directions, we
turned down Post Oak Drive and then into a chic-
looking shopping center. At the end of the row of
stores there was a blue awning that said "Tony's."

As I stopped the car, a young lad in white shirt
and black pants opened the door and said, "Good
evening, sir!" Then, recognizing Laurie, he hur-
ried around to open the door on her side and said,
"Hello, Miss Jeppsen. Sure sorry to hear about
your dad."

"Thank you, Miles," she said. And Miles drove
off to park the car.

We were greeted similarly by the doorman and
the maître d', who led us past richly paneled walls
to a white-covered table set with gleaming silver
and china, Baccarat crystal and freshly cut roses.

"Nice place," I commented.

"Yes, it is a nice place," she said. "If you hadn't

been properly dressed, I wouldn't have brought you here."

After a full day of work, my glen-plaid suit was beginning to take on a few wrinkles, so I said, "Personally, I don't feel all that well dressed."

"Yes, but you have a tie. This is one place where you need a tie. I mean *need* one. No exceptions."

"Not for anyone?"

"Not for anyone. One night Frank Sinatra was politely ushered out because he wouldn't wear one. How about that?" Once again that merry laugh.

The waiter brought our drinks: my usual Scotch on the rocks and a Vodka martini for Laurie. They were both in Texas-size glasses.

Then it was my turn to get serious. "Laurie, we were talking about money before. How did your dad feel about money?"

"As far as dad was concerned, life was all a big game of Monopoly. He used his power to make money, and he used his money to make more power. He was a doer, not a spender. To him, money was just one of the pieces on the board."

"How about your brother? Tell me more about him."

"Randy? He's just the opposite. I hate to say it, but he's the kind who takes—takes and never gives anything back."

"Does he still live at home?"

"No. He's got an apartment at the Woodway. A real bachelor pad—looks like one of those photo essays in *Playboy*. I haven't been there in a couple of years; neither has anyone else in the family, as far as I know."

I made a mental note to pay young Randy Jeppsen a visit when I got a chance. Then I said, "I gather your mother didn't exactly appreciate my visit today. But I guess I can't blame her."

"No, this has been a rough time for her. Especially on top of everything else. I don't think she could have handled it without Roger."

"Roger? I know he takes over the company now, but...." I stopped. Something suddenly occurred to me.

Laurie confirmed my suspicion. "He just may be taking over more than that. Roger's wife died about ten years ago, and since then... well, he was always fond of mommy, so it seemed kind of natural for them to gravitate toward each other. You know by now that daddy wasn't exactly a faithful husband."

At a signal from Laurie, the waiter brought a second round of drinks and took our dinner order. To Laurie, this whole game of Texas musical beds seemed like a normal series of events. To me, it only raised more questions. I sensed I was getting embroiled in more than I wanted to.

"Anyway," Laurie went on, "mommy and Roger just may get married—after a time, of course. Meanwhile, he's a staunch family friend, the way he's always been."

"I see." More pieces of the puzzle were beginning to fall into place.

Laurie didn't seem to sense what I was thinking. "Roger has made all the plans for the funeral, too. It'll be a simple memorial service, naturally. Why don't you stop by?"

"Well, I don't think that would be quite appropriate would it? I mean, after today. . . ."

"Oh, don't worry about that. As I said, mommy wasn't herself this afternoon. You can understand that, can't you?"

"Sure I can, but still. . . ."

"Look, tomorrow's Saturday. Roger can't expect you to work weekends, too. It's at St. Luke's at two o'clock. I'll expect to see you there." Then she reached across the table and took my hand. "Fact is, Johnny, I'll expect to see *lots* more of you."

The waiter brought our dinners. The food matched the surroundings: it was delicious. We ate mostly in silence, but kept looking at each other. I'm sure we were both thinking about the same thing, and it didn't have anything to do with murder.

As I drove Laurie home and then headed back to the Shamrock, I was also thinking that Laurie seemed to have a way of getting what she wanted.

9

WHEN I GOT TO MY ROOM, the little red light on the telephone was blinking, so I called downstairs for messages. "A Miss Lisa Wallace phoned you at 5:45," the operator said, and she gave me the number.

I dialed, and Lisa's throaty "Hello" came over the wire almost immediately.

"Hi, Lisa," I said. "It's Johnny. I hear you called me earlier this evening."

"Yes. Frankly, I was hoping you'd take me out to dinner."

"Sorry about that. How about tomorrow?"

"Sure thing. Pick me up at seven." She gave me an address on Montrose Avenue.

"Great. I'll look forward to it. See you then." I started to hang up.

"Wait a minute. I've got to talk to you. And some of it can't wait."

"Oh? What's up?"

"Well, when Roger came back to the office after the news conference, he seemed pretty satisfied with himself. I gather it went over very well."

"Yes, it did. I told him I thought he did a super job."

"Thanks to your speech, no doubt. Anyway,

then he got a phone call from Randy. I don't know what they talked about—I didn't try to listen in—but whatever it was, it sure got Roger upset."

"Upset? How?"

"I don't know. But Roger was shaking almost the way he did when the call about Bart's murder came in at the Dome the other night. That Randy is a no-good twerp. Have you talked to him yet?"

"My God, Lisa, I've just got started on this thing, remember? I didn't even get through the news conference till four o'clock this afternoon."

"Well, I just thought maybe you could have spent the rest of the day doing what *I* asked you to."

"I did, dammit!" Lisa was pushing me more than I like being pushed. But then I realized that it was guilt that was driving her—guilt over her waning feelings for Jeppsen. So, in a softer tone, I told her about my visit with Cynthia. I didn't discuss my dinner with Laurie.

Lisa's tone softened too. "Well, that's some progress. Thanks, Johnny. But do you think you could talk to Randy this evening? Something's going on there, and it scares the hell out of me."

I looked at my watch. It read 9:45 and I'd been up since five. "Isn't it rather late?"

"Not for Randy," she said. "He never gets out of bed till noon, so he's up most of the night. At least that's what I hear. *Please*, Johnny."

I sighed. "Okay, Lisa. I'll give it a go."

"Thanks," she said. "You can tell me all about it tomorrow evening. See you at seven."

THE WOODWAY WAS a modern hexagonal-shaped building just beyond the West Loop. I'd considered phoning Randy first, but then decided I'd do just as well making it a surprise visit. Scanning the names on the mailboxes in the lobby, I finally found the one that said, "Randall Jeppsen—604." Randall? Then I remembered: Lathrop had told me that was Cynthia Jeppsen's maiden name.

I rode the sleek elevator up to the sixth floor and walked along the deep-carpeted hallway to 604. Even as I approached, I could hear loud disco-type music coming from inside the apartment. I had no idea at that moment what the neighbors thought of young Mr. Jeppsen, but I decided instantly that if I ever moved to Houston, I'd find someplace else to live.

I rang the buzzer. No answer. I leaned on it harder and longer. Finally the music was turned down and a skinny young girl, about Laurie's age, opened the door. Her bright red hair hung in loose strings, and she didn't seem to notice that she was naked.

"Yeah?" she said. "What is it?"

I blinked, but tried to sound casual. "Excuse me, is Randy Jeppsen home?"

She still held the door open; but made no attempt to invite me in. "No, he had to go back to the club. They were having some kind of trouble there."

"Excuse me," I repeated. "What club?"

"*His* club, of course, dummy. The Wahoo Lounge."

This was getting more confusing by the second! "Excuse me," I said for the third time, "but can I come in for just a minute?"

She shrugged. "Sure, I guess so. But if you want a party, it'll cost you fifty dollars." She stepped aside for me to enter, then closed the door behind me. She sat down casually in a suede armchair and said, "Would you like a smoke?" It was obvious she wasn't referring to ordinary tobacco.

I sat down in a chair on the opposite side of the room. With its chrome-and-glass furniture, mirrored ceiling and garish lighting, Randy Jeppsen's apartment was indeed, as Laurie had said, the kind of pad you usually see only in X-rated movies.

"Look, Miss..."

"Lemoyne. Moira Lemoyne."

"Miss Lemoyne. No, thanks, I don't care for a smoke right now, and I'm not looking for a party. My name's Johnny McCoy, and I need to talk with Randy."

"You're not a cop, are you?" She started to reach for a faded blue robe behind her.

"No, I'm not a cop. I'm just a friend of the Jeppsen family, and I'm doing some PR work for the company. When do you think Randy will be home?"

She let the robe fall to the floor and gave me another shrug. "Who knows? With the kind of trouble he's been having lately, it could be hours."

"Tell me about this club, Miss Lemoyne."

"The Wahoo? It's out on Richmond. Just off Gessner. An all-night spot like all the rest of 'em. Topless, bottomless, couch-dancing. The whole bit."

I began to see that Randy Jeppsen was not a

complete idler. But he was involved in activities his family apparently didn't know about—and surely wouldn't approve of.

"How long has Randy owned this club?" I asked.

"Oh, a couple of years. I've only worked there for a month, since I came over from New Orleans. This is my night off—only because Randy planned to spend it with me. And on a Friday, too! Shit! I could have made a couple of hundred if I'd stayed on the job. You know what I mean?"

"Yes, I think I do, Miss Lemoyne." I got up to go. "Thanks for the information."

She stood, too, and walked toward me. "Sure you don't want a party?" She gazed thoughtfully at my body. "I just might cut it to twenty-five dollars."

"Thanks anyway. Good night."

The September evening was warm, but I shivered a little as I got back into the Cutlass.

10

LIKE TONY'S RESTAURANT, where Laurie and I had dined earlier in the evening, the Wahoo Lounge was located in a shopping center. There was a self-service gas station on the corner, with an orange sign that said "Save More With Sav-Mor." Next to that was an all-night hamburger joint. Then a Stop-and-Go Market. Then an establishment called Adult Books Unlimited, whose windows displayed a variety of vibrators and other similar devices along with racks of magazines. Then a modeling studio. Finally, beyond the X-tra Attractions Theater, I came upon the Wahoo Lounge. It was bathed in a rainbow of lights.

The girl at the door was far more modestly dressed than Moira Lemoyne had been: she wore a G-string. "There's a two-drink minimum," she said. "That'll be ten dollars please."

I forked over the ten and stepped inside. Immediately another girl—similarly attired in a G-string—sidled up to me and said, "Would you like a couch in the back, fella? That's where the real action is."

"No thanks," I said. "The bar'll be fine."

I walked to the bar at the far side and handed the bearded young bartender the two yellow slips of paper I'd been given at the door. "Let me have a double Scotch, please," I said.

The bartender stared at me as if I'd just arrived from Mars. "Look, buddy, don't get smart. Those chits are for beer. You want a double Scotch, that'll be ten bucks more."

I knew I wasn't going to enjoy my visit to the Wahoo Lounge very much, anyway, but thought I might as well make my stay as palatable as possible. I pulled out another ten and dropped it onto the bar. "Now, could I have a double Scotch, please?"

The bartender shrugged, poured for a moment from a nondescript bottle and put a pale yellow drink down in front of me.

"Thanks," I said, trying to be polite. "I'm looking for Randy Jeppsen. Is he here?"

"Who wants to know?"

The whole scene was beginning to get on my nerves. I grabbed the bartender by his unwashed T-shirt and yanked him against the bar. "*I* do," I said. "The name's Johnny McCoy."

The kid's eyes bugged. "Okay, okay. Lay off, will ya? I'll go tell him you're here."

As the bartender stepped through a small hallway, presumably to announce my presence, I began to look around the place. The customers were almost all male, of course, but of varying ages. Some were dressed in cowboy boots and blue jeans, others in sport coats with open-neck shirts. One group of a half-dozen conventioneers in business suits, obviously drunk, had name tags on their lapels.

Behind the bar, on an elevated stage, a girl was

dancing to music that kept blaring out of the two loudspeakers at the sides. The sounds of heavy breathing and an occasional "Ooh-aah" came from the couch at the far side. The girl on the stage took off her G-string and began twirling it in one hand. She winked at me invitingly. I looked away.

Meanwhile, other G-stringed girls were everywhere, edging their way through the crowd, patting, and being patted by the various customers.

One of them cuddled up close to me and whispered, "Hi! Want a good time?"

I removed her hand from my crotch and said, "Thanks, not tonight."

Finally, thank God, Randy Jeppsen appeared out of the hallway at the end of the bar.

"Hello, Randy," I said. "I'm Johnny McCoy."

"Yeah, I know. I saw you at the Dome the night my dad got knocked off." There was no sorrow in the way he said it.

"That's right. Can I talk to you for a minute...in private?"

"Sure. What's to lose? Come on back to the office."

The closet-size cubicle that Randy referred to as his office was as seedy as the rest of the place. The desk was a beat-up table, the two straight chairs were unpainted, and the file cabinet was one of those expandable cardboard folders that you can buy in any five and dime. I'd learned that Randy Jeppsen liked to spend money, but obviously he spent it elsewhere.

He sat down behind the card table, motioned me into the other chair, and said, "Okay, McCoy. What's on your mind?"

"A lot of things," I began. "For one, I'm trying to help find out who killed your dad. I thought you might be able to help. Any ideas?"

He laughed in my face. "How the hell should I know? Dad may have been a knight in shining armor to some people, but a lot of others hated his guts."

"That last category just might include you," I pointed out.

"Hell, yes! That's no secret to anybody. Neither is the fact that I wasn't his favorite, either. But I didn't kill him, if that's what you're getting at."

I decided to change the subject. "Did he know about your little enterprise here—the Wahoo Lounge?"

"Hell, no. But he wouldn't have understood anyway. All he ever cared about was Jeppsen Tool. People in the oil patch don't even know any other business exists. You'll find that out soon enough, if you haven't already."

"But *why*, Randy? I know this kind of club is legal these days, but. . . well, God knows there are lots of other businesses you could have got into."

"I'll tell you why, McCoy. Two reasons." He ticked them off on his fingers. "One, it's as far as I could get from Jeppsen Oil Tool. That's reason enough. And two, it brings in bread—*lots* of bread."

"Then why have you been bugging your mother for money?"

He stared at me, and his weak face took on a look of cruelty. "Who the hell told you about that?"

"It's pretty common knowledge," I said noncommittally. "But you haven't answered the question."

He stood up. "And why do I have to answer your question, McCoy? Why don't you just stick to your PR work and leave me the hell alone?"

I remained seated. "Of course, I can do that, Randy," I said softly. "But somebody's going to ask you those questions, if they haven't already."

He snorted. "You mean Mendez. Yeah, he came by last night. So what?"

"Then let me ask you something else," I went on. "Lisa Wallace said you called Roger Lathrop today and got him pretty well shook up. What was that all about?"

He remained standing. "Shit, I just asked him when I could start drawing my share of the estate, that's all. What's wrong with that?"

"Nothing, maybe. But why did you have to come down here tonight? Especially with Moira Lemoyne planning to spend the evening in your apartment. Are you in some kind of trouble, Randy?"

"No dammit!" He put his hands on his hips, trying to look tough. "Now look, McCoy," he shouted. "That's about all I'm going to take from you, and you can just...."

At that moment the phone rang. Randy picked up the receiver and said, "Yeah." There was a pause. "Just a minute."

He looked back toward me and finished the sentence: "... get the hell out of here."

"Okay," I said. "Maybe we'll talk some more later." And I left.

But standing outside the office in that dim hallway, I hesitated. It's not exactly polite to listen in on other people's conversations, but I listened anyway.

"Look, Marty," I heard Randy say, "I'll have the money in just a few days. . . . Yeah, I know I'm two months overdue, but. . . . Okay, okay, I'll get it by the end of the week. . . . Yes, you can count on it." I heard the slamming of the receiver and then one final word from Randy: "Shit!"

As I stepped through the Wahoo Lounge's front door, I took a deep breath of the late-night air. Oh, well, I thought again, at least I can sleep late in the morning.

Meanwhile, I was getting some answers.

But each answer only led to more questions.

11

BY ONE-THIRTY THE NEXT AFTERNOON, St. Luke's
hallowed sanctuary was jammed. Bart Jeppsen's
mourners filled the main level and overflowed
onto the balcony above, pressing into the area occupied by two dozen white-robed choir members.
Thousands more people of all ages, mostly just
curiosity seekers, ignored the Keep off the Grass
signs and camped on the manicured lawn outside.
Television cameras mounted atop white vans
filmed the proceedings along Westheimer Road, as
long black limousines disgorged the notables, including Houston's affable young mayor and
Texas's silver-maned governor, who had flown in
that morning in his private jet. The half-dozen extra policemen who were there for the occasion
seemed totally unable to control the hooting traffic.

Laurie had told me that it would be a "simple"
memorial service. Maybe, by River Oaks standards, it was. To me, the whole scene looked like
the old newsreels I'd seen of Rudolph Valentino's
funeral in Hollywood.

But she was right about the service itself. At
precisely 2:00 P.M., Reverend Gaylord Seale
stepped up to the pulpit and read a brief psalm,

which was followed by a soft hymn from the choir and then the Reverend Mr. Seale's glowing eulogy. "Yes," he intoned in conclusion, "Bart Jeppsen no longer walks among us. But by his lifetime of good works—and by the grace of our Father and our Lord Jesus Christ—he lives forever." There was a short prayer and then it was over.

As the members of the family walked out with heads bowed, Laurie spied me along the aisle near the back. "I'll wait for you outside," she whispered.

I ducked out as quickly as I could and found her standing on the steps, accepting the awkward words of condolence being mumbled on all sides.

"Let's get the hell out of here," she said. "Fast. And as far away as possible."

I began to wonder whether more time with Laurie might provide new clues to Bart Jeppsen's murder, or whether I didn't really give a damn one way or the other. So I simply said, "I'm with you," and led her around the corner where I'd parked the Cutlass.

As I turned on the ignition, I said, "Where to?"

"Like I said, as far away as possible. To another planet if you can arrange it."

Suddenly I had an idea. "I can't quite fix that, but I do have an airplane out at Hobby. We could go for a ride if you want."

Laurie brightened immediately. "Hey, that'd be neat! Let's!"

"You're on."

As we headed toward the Gulf Freeway, I said, "Laurie, I know how you must feel. But that was a beautiful service."

"Yes, I guess it was. But as far as I'm concerned, there's no such thing as a good funeral. They all seem like pagan rituals. You know what I mean?"

"No, what?"

"Well, I'll just bet that a couple of thousand years from now people will look back and call us pagans the same way we think of the people who worshiped fire or wooden idols."

"Is that what they teach you at Rice?"

She laughed. "No, they all think I'm crazy. But then, I don't agree with everything they try to promote. They don't have all the answers, either."

"I guess nobody does, Laurie. But from what I've heard, Rice is a mighty fine school."

"Sure it is. One of the best anywhere. But almost everything they teach has to do with the past—what *has* happened. If you want to know what *will* happen, you have to learn it from some place like the Center."

"The Center? What's that?"

"The Enlightened Research Center. That's where I go to get the real answers—most of them, anyway."

"For instance."

"For instance, UFOs. They're for real. Also natural healing. There's something to that, too, you know. Like if I wake up in the morning with a headache, I just think yellow. That cures it."

"Run that by me again."

"Yellow. The color. Same way that if you're angry or frustrated, you see red. That's where the expression comes from. To fix it, you think blue."

None of this made much sense to me, but I didn't

feel like arguing. So all I said was, "What does all
that have to do with funerals?"

"It's another part of the same thing. When people are buried, their spirit can get trapped inside
the body. If they're cremated, the spirit is freed to
go on to bigger and better things. That's what it's
all about." She paused for a moment. "At least,
that's *one* good thing about daddy's death. They'll
never lock him in a grave."

I was beginning to find the whole conversation a
bit eerie. With a normal middle-America up-
bringing—and now an almost-normal Eastern
Establishment adulthood—such theories had
never concerned me. And I frankly didn't want
them to. But who knows?

Anyway, it showed me still another side of
Laurie's character. There was far greater depth to
it than I'd first thought. Her moods seemed to
swing like a pendulum from gay to serious and
back again, regardless of the events taking place
around her. I even began to wonder how *I* was
beginning to feel about *her*. She was well past the
age of consent, of course, but. . . .

We finally pulled into Grundy Aviation's dusty
driveway and parked. Stepping into the office, I
could see that the motherly looking woman who'd
greeted me that first evening was back on the job.

"Hello, Mrs. Grundy," I said. "I'm terribly sorry
about what happened to your husband."

Martha Grundy sighed and her large bosom
heaved. "So am I, Mr. McCoy. It was tough enough
paying the rent on this place while Herb was here,
not to mention the bank loans on the aircraft. I
just don't know how we'll manage now."

"I'm sure it's not easy," I said. "But maybe things'll work out okay. I sure hope so."

"So do I, Mr. McCoy. So do I." Again, her ample bosom moved up and down behind the glass counter.

"Mrs. Grundy, Miss Jeppsen and I are going for a ride—just a local flight over the city. Was my Bonanza topped off after I came in the other evening?"

"I think so. Just a minute and I'll make sure." She turned to a hook on the wall behind her and fingered through some gas tickets. "Yes, here it is: Bonanza 3682L, 58.7 gallons. If you want, I can just hold it till you're ready to leave town."

"That's fine, Mrs. Grundy. Maybe I'll let you give it a twenty-five-hour check, too. It's just about due for one."

I could see she knew I was lying, that I was just trying to give her a little extra business. She blinked back a tear and said, "Certainly, Mr. McCoy. Thank you."

Laurie and I walked outside into the windswept parking area in front of the hangar. I untied the Bonanza, checked the gas and oil as I always do, and we climbed aboard. Moments later, we got our takeoff clearance and roared down the runway toward the cloudless sky. As always, like every pilot who ever earned his wings, I felt that familiar thrill as the wheels lifted off the runway and seconds later tucked themselves neatly into the wing-roots.

I recently saw a sixty-six-year-old grandmother being interviewed on TV. She had just learned to fly. When the reporter asked her why, and what she so enjoyed about it, she said, "It's better than sex." Well, I won't go that far, but I know what she means.

For the next half hour we swooped over the far-flung reaches of Houston. Laurie was like a kid at the circus. I enjoyed it, too, especially because *she* enjoyed it and also because of the glorious view. Spread out under the gleaming sun, Houston looked for all the world like a giant Disneyland.

Finally, I turned the Bonanza's nose back toward Hobby, entered the pattern and lowered the gear. Moments later, the wheels kissed the ground.

Laurie looked at me intently, as she had repeatedly during the flight. "That was just wonderful, Johnny!"

I parked in the same spot in front of the Grundy Aviation hangar. We got out, and I began to loop the chains through the tie-down rigs.

Just then, a Cessna Skyplane pulled in alongside us. Grundy's freckle-faced helicopter pilot climbed out and said, "Here, let me give you a hand."

"Oh, hi," I said. "Sure. Thanks."

As we finished tying down the airplane, I said, "I haven't officially met you. My name's Johnny McCoy." I held out my hand.

He shook it and grinned. "I know. I'm Jack Hamilton. Chief pilot, instructor, mechanic, gas filler-upper and office boy."

I grinned back. "I know how it is in your business. And I guess Mrs. Grundy is going to need all your talents now more than ever."

His face clouded over. "Yes, I'm afraid she is.

That was a hell of a thing that happened the other night.''

"It sure was. Say, top off the tanks for me when you get a chance, will you? And I told Mrs. Grundy I'd want an oil change, too. You know, a regular twenty-five-hour check.''

"Sure thing, no problem. I'll take care of it Monday morning, if that's okay. About how much gas will you need?''

"Only a few gallons. Laurie Jeppsen and I have just been doing a little sight-seeing for the past half hour.''

He laughed. "Joyriding, huh? I've been doing the same thing in the Skyplane.'' He shook his head. "Even on my time off, I've got to get into the sky. That's a pilot for you.''

I laughed with him. "I guess we're all the same.''

Laurie and I waved goodbye, got back into the Cutlass and headed north toward the city.

Her cool fingers stroked my cheek gently. "You're quite a guy, Johnny.''

I grinned. "You're not so bad yourself.''

"Hey, if you liked Tony's, wait till you see the place I've picked out for tonight.''

"Sorry, honey, I've got other plans for the evening.'' She took her hand away abruptly. "Just business,'' I added.

"Oh, that's different.'' Her fingers continued their stroking. "Then how about stopping by your hotel for a while. You could buy me a drink and...well, I wouldn't mind getting out of this funeral garb for a few minutes.'' She was giving me that intent look again. "Or a few hours, either.''

It was damned inviting, but I said, "Really, Laurie, I don't think that'd be a good idea. Not just now, anyway."

She continued to stroke me. "You're sure?"

"Yes, I'm sure! Now, cut it out!"

But as I dropped Laurie off at her River Oaks home and felt the taste of her lips before leaving, I wasn't so sure at all.

12

"HELLO, STRANGER," Lisa said as she opened the door. "Come on in."

"Thanks. It's good to see you."

I wasn't kidding. In a tailored beige dress that accentuated her dark hair and trim figure, Lisa did look good. And the tasteful furnishings of her apartment matched their owner: simple, direct, no ostentation, but very attractive.

"Would you like a drink?" she asked.

"Sure. Scotch on the rocks would be fine."

She mixed us a couple of Scotches—mine a shade or two darker than her own—and we sat down on a soft white sofa along the wall.

Lisa tucked her long legs under her and faced me. "Well," she said, lifting her glass, "tell me how you've been faring in our big, bad city."

I laughed. "It's big, all right. But not so bad. Not now, anyway."

She smiled. "Thank you, kind sir! But seriously, tell me what you've been doing. I'm really interested, you know."

"Yes, of course I know, Lisa. And I know why. So, okay, I'll tell you."

And I did. The whole story—that is, all except for Laurie's direct invitation. Lisa listened without interruption. She just sat there, looking at me, sipping her drink.

When I'd finished, she said, "Wow! You *have* been busy. That's good. We've got a lot to talk about." She put down her empty glass. "But what say we do it over dinner?"

"Good idea," I agreed. "But you be the guide. I'm still a tourist."

Lisa directed us to a small French restaurant not far from her apartment. It was nowhere near as posh as Tony's, but it was loaded with charm. A rotund man handed us menus and placed a bottle of wine in the center of the checkered tablecloth covering the round table.

"There you are, Miss Wallace," he said. "Enjoy!"

"Thank you, Pierre. I'll have my usual. And so will Mr. McCoy. Okay with you, Johnny? You haven't lived till you've tasted Pierre's Poulard Marseilles. The sauce'll knock you out."

"Fine with me. I can see you've been here before."

"Ah yes," Pierre said, nodding. "Miss Wallace is one of our favorite customers. And I do hope you enjoy it, Mr. McCoy." He bowed and reached for the menus.

"I'll keep mine for a while, if you don't mind," Lisa said. "I think better with a piece of paper in my hand." Pierre bowed again and waddled back toward the kitchen.

Lisa reached in her purse and brought out a pencil. "Now," she said, turning over the menu, "let's see what we've got."

"We've got a mess, Lisa. That's what we've got."

"No, I mean possible suspects. We have to find out who killed Bart, Johnny."

"I thought that was Mendez's job. Ours is to enjoy dinner."

She looked up and frowned. "I thought we went through all that the other night, Johnny. Look, you've come up with some important information. And from what I hear, you and Mendez aren't exactly working as buddies on this thing."

I grinned. "That's true enough."

"All right, then. It's up to *us* to do what we can."

I sighed. "Okay, Miss Marple. Start writing. The first obvious suspect is Cynthia."

"Right. She gets rid of Bart without having to divorce him, which she didn't want to do. And after the dust settles, she marries Roger. They live happily ever after."

"But we have no way of proving anything," I protested.

"Of course not, silly. All we're doing now is listing the suspects. Who's next?"

"Well, Randy, obviously."

"Right again. He never got along with Bart—he even admits that—and now he's in some kind of trouble we didn't know about before. With Bart out of the way, he comes into a big bundle—something he can borrow against, anyway—so now he pays off his debts and he's clean."

At that moment Pierre brought our food. The

sauce was excellent, and for a short while we ate in silence.

Then, between mouthfuls of chicken, Lisa said, "Let's not forget Laurie." She picked up her pencil and made another note on the back of the menu. "Laurie may not be in hock the way Randy is, but she comes in to the same amount of money."

That idea made no sense to me at all, but I didn't want to interrupt Lisa's train of thought. "Okay, then let's not forget Roger," I said.

"By all means, let's not. He's the partner and he's fooling around with the boss's wife—that's something I always suspected but never really knew. Anyway, now he takes over the company *and* the wife. How about that!"

"It's certainly possible," I admitted.

Lisa suddenly snapped her fingers. "Say, how about this: Roger and Cynthia were in it together! Maybe that's the answer," she said triumphantly.

"That could be, too, of course. You know it's funny, Lisa—funny strange, not funny ha-ha."

"What is?"

"Well, when I worked on that Chip Lloyd case in New York, everybody had the opportunity but nobody had a motive. Here it's exactly the opposite: none of these people was out at the rig that night, so whoever did it must have paid somebody to do it. But it seems that everybody had a reason to do just that!"

"So which one of 'em did it?" Lisa looked over her list. "You know, if I had to bet on somebody right now, I'd pick Randy. That little bastard is just no damn good. Like bugging Roger, asking for his father's money now, even before the funeral service. Can you imagine that?''

"Yes, I can, Lisa. I can't condone it, but I can imagine it, especially when he's under the gun the way he seems to be right now. I mean, he was scared when that phone call came in from Marty—whoever that is.''

Lisa put down the menu and dropped her pencil on the tablecloth. Her eyes widened. "Oh, God, Johnny!'' She looked almost physically ill.

"For heaven's sake, Lisa, what's the matter? Are you all right?''

"No, I'm not all right, Johnny, and neither are you. I hope I'm wrong but . . . .''

"Lisa, what are you talking about?''

"Look, Johnny, as you said, you're still a tourist—the new kid on the block. You haven't been reading the papers around here lately, but they say there's a whole new mob that's moved into town—mostly from Chicago, I think. They're the ones who really control the strip joints and the porno book stores and the X-rated movies and all the rest.''

"That happens everywhere, Lisa. So what?''

"So the big shot who's top man in the whole outfit, according to the papers, is a guy named Marty. Marty Angel. The district attorney has been after him ever since he moved here.''

"Oh-oh. I see what you mean.''

"Jesus, Johnny, if Randy's mixed up with him and you get mixed up with Randy. . . . Oh, God, what have I got you into?'' She was actually shaking. "Maybe you were right before, Johnny. Let's

forget the whole works and let Mendez worry
about it. I'm scared.''

I reached across the table and covered her hand
with mine. ''And as you said, Lisa, we have a
responsibility in this thing, too. Somehow, I feel
I've got to see it through.''

''Okay, Johnny. But don't let anything happen
to you, too. *Please*.''

''I won't. I promise.''

We finished our meal in silence. Then Lisa said,
''Johnny, I'm scared. Take me home, will you?''

''Of course.'' I paid the check and we left.

During the short drive home, Lisa sat close to
me, saying nothing. When we finally arrived at
her Montrose Avenue apartment house, she
looked at me. ''Will you come upstairs for a
while?'' she asked.

''Gee, I don't know.''

''Just for a nightcap, I mean.''

''Well, sure, why not?''

I was beginning to like Lisa more all the time.

13

THE NEXT DAY, Sunday, the insistent clang of the telephone on my bedside table intruded at 7:30 A.M. I finally picked up the receiver on the fourth ring.

It was Lisa. "Are you awake?" she asked.

"I am now."

"Sorry about that. Then you haven't read the paper yet."

"No. I haven't done *anything* yet, dammit!"

"Hold on, Johnny. I'm sorry to wake you up. Really. But there's something in this morning's *Post* that you should see—two things, actually. And both could be important."

"Like what?"

"Like about Bart's murder and about Marty Angel."

I sat up straight. "You're right, Lisa. That could be important. I'll get hold of a paper as quick as I can and take a look."

"Will you call me back after you've read it?"

"Sure, sure. Sorry I barked at you. I'll talk to you later."

I immediately dialed room service. I ordered breakfast and told them to send up a copy of the *Houston Post* along with it.

A half hour later, freshly showered and shaved, I was scanning the paper between mouthfuls of scrambled eggs and bacon. For once, I was concentrating more on the news than I was on my breakfast.

The two items Lisa had referred to were not hard to find. One was a full-page story opposite the editorial page, titled, "Is Houston America's New sin city?" It was by-lined Howard Ketchum. I decided that maybe a visit with Mr. Ketchum might be in order.

Meanwhile, I was engrossed in the article. In crisp prose, it described the growth of sexually oriented businesses in the city: massage parlors, nude modeling studios, X-rated movie theaters, strip joints and so-called adult bookstores. And there were photos of each, including a shot of the Wahoo Lounge. "Most, if not all, of these establishments," the article went on, "are fronts for prostitution."

Then there were quotes from some of the leading citizenry, including the mayor, the chief of police, the bishop of the Catholic Church and the executive director of the Chamber of Commerce. All expressed dismay, but said they were helpless to do anything about it. One business leader was quoted as saying: "If people would just stop patronizing these places, they'd dry up and blow away."

Finally, there was a separate insert occupying the bottom third of the page. The subhead read: "Who's Behind It All?" And it was this part of the article that drew my closest attention.

"No one can be certain who heads up Houston's pornography industry," it began, "but surely it isn't by native Texans." Then there was a run-down on some of the mobsters who had recently moved in from New York, Chicago, Los Angeles and Las Vegas. Howard Ketchum was careful not to make specific accusations, but the implication was clear. And the name most prominently mentioned was that of Marty Angel.

The other item Lisa had indicated was even easier to find. It was an entire special section of the paper titled, "Bart Jeppsen: How He Lived, How He Died." The cover carried the same square-jawed portrait that hung in the foyer of the Jeppsen plant.

Inside were photos of Bart Jeppsen as a cherubic young child; Bart Jeppsen as the gangling president of the student body at Rice; Bart Jeppsen as an all-American football hero; Bart Jeppsen as a proud groom, with a radiant Cynthia Randall Jeppsen on his arm; and a half-dozen later shots of Bart Jeppsen meeting with various heads of state around the world. The text carried the entire story of his life—a fitting tribute to a giant of American free enterprise.

One other small article, I was pleased to see, was headlined: "Jeppsen Oil Tool Company—the Future." It covered Friday's news conference in detail and carried the gist of the press release I had prepared.

But it was the final page of the section that interested me most. It was headlined simply: "Who Killed Bart Jeppsen?" All of the known facts were discussed, but little was said about the many suspects. Lieutenant Mendez was quoted as saying, "The Houston Police Department is engaging all its forces behind this full-scale effort. We do not as yet know who committed this foul deed. But he will be brought to justice."

Centered at the bottom of the page was a single photo, captioned: "Box of Mystery, Dealer of Death." It showed a replica of the case with the used bit that Bart had carried aboard the helicopter that evening, the case that apparently had contained the bomb that killed him. The border around the photo was made up of a series of small question marks.

It left me with questions of my own.

I picked up the phone and dialed Lisa's number. She answered immediately. "Johnny, is that you?"

"It's me, all right. Yes, that paper had a lot to chew on."

"Did you see the story about the porn business in Houston? And the picture of the Wahoo Lounge?"

"Of course I did, Lisa. As I said, that sort of thing may be new to Houston, but it's been around up north for years."

"Well, what did I tell you about Marty Angel? He's got to be who Randy was talking to on the phone when you were there Friday night."

"Yes, you're probably right."

"Then, don't you think maybe I was right last evening, too—that maybe you ought to back off? I mean, this guy Angel doesn't seem like anybody to fool with."

"Dammit, Lisa! First you push me to jump into this thing feet first. Now you try to get me to back out. What *do* you want, anyway?"

She started to sob softly. "Oh, Johnny, I just don't know. I really don't. Yes, I want Bart's murderer caught. You know that. But I don't want to see you killed, too."

I could see she was confused and with good reason. "Take it easy, Lisa. I'll be okay."

"All right. But you take it easy, too."

"That's more like it," I said. "You want to know what I think the next step is?"

"What?" She sounded more like the efficient secretary now.

"Well, we've been concentrating on the obvious suspects—the people with a real motive, the ones who might have paid somebody to load that bomb on the chopper."

"So? Isn't that logical?"

"Sure it is...up to a point. But I'm still wondering who did it, who actually put the bomb in that box. That's something we've almost forgotten."

"Okay, Sherlock. How do we find that out?"

"I don't know how. But I think I know where. It all happened at the rig that night, so that's the place to look. I think maybe I'll call Jack Hamilton and see if he can fly me out there again this afternoon."

"Okay if I go with you?"

I thought for a moment. I certainly didn't want to get Lisa involved in any danger, but I couldn't see where a trip to the rig on this occasion would put her in jeopardy.

So I said, "Sure. I'll make the arangements and pick you up in a half hour."

It wasn't until much later that I learned how wrong I could have been.

14

PRIVATE PILOTS DO most of their flying on Sundays, so the facilities that serve them—fixed base operators, as they're commonly known in the trade—are always busy on the Sabbath. Invariably, there's a gay bustle of activity around the place.

But Grundy Aviation was an exception. There was no leather-jacketed, part-time instructors checking off logbooks. No potbellied businessmen, grinning like schoolboys, celebrating their first solo flights. Not even the inevitable loiterers swapping tales of their latest air exploits. As always, every time I'd been there, Grundy Aviation was about as noisy as the public library.

Martha Grundy was the only person on the premises. Seated behind a desk in the back, she was checking the books. Her head was shaking from side to side, her heavy bosom moving vertically in unison, as she fingered through the ledger in front of her.

"Hi, Mrs. Grundy," I called out. "Is Jack ready with the chopper?"

"Oh, hello, Mr. McCoy, Miss Wallace. No, he isn't back yet. I'm sure he will be any minute, though. Why don't you folks come in and sit down. It won't be long."

"But I thought you said he'd be back by now. Where is he?"

"Well, as you can see, he didn't have any students scheduled for this morning—or for most of the afternoon, either, for that matter. That's why, when you phoned earlier, I was able to schedule him to fly you out to the rig. Anyway, Jack has a girl friend in Corpus Christi. And you know how young people are these days." Again her large bosom heaved. "So after he finished with his two students yesterday, he flew down to spend the night with her. But he promised to be back by eleven." Her eyes clouded. "Heck I'm *happy* when he uses the ship. At least he helps pay for the insurance."

All that made sense. But I'd learned from long, and sometimes painful, experience that private airplanes rarely operate on schedule. "Are there any restaurants in the neighborhood? Maybe Miss Wallace and I can have a bite to eat in the meantime.

"Certainly, Mr. McCoy. The Ranch House is a nice little place. It's just a half mile down Telephone Road. If you want to wait there, I'll be glad to tell Jack as soon as he gets in. I'm sure you won't have to wait long."

For once, a private airplane did make it almost on time. Lisa and I were just biting into our hamburgers when a dilapidated Volkswagen pulled up outside and Jack Hamilton walked in the door. As usual, he was casually dressed in sport shirt and slacks, and his curly red hair needed combing.

He saw us and waved. "Hi! Martha said you'd be here. Mind if I join you?"

"Sure. Have a seat."

He walked over and nonchalantly leaned against the back of a chair. "Martha says you want to pay another visit to the rig. If it'll help find out who loaded a bomb on that chopper, I'm all for it."

"That's the idea," I said. "But tell me. . . have things always been this slow around your place on Sundays?"

"I'm afraid so. Business has never been what it should, and I can't see it getting any better now."

"But why, Jack? What's been the trouble? I thought aviation was booming around Houston, like everything else."

"It is—for most outfits. But Herb was never much of a businessman. A hell of a fine pilot, yes. And a terrific guy. But never a salesman. You're a PR man, so you know how it is. Customers have to be cultivated. Herb just didn't know how—and didn't have the money to hire anyone else to do it." He spread his hands. "So there you have it. If it hadn't been for a few regular clients like Jeppsen Oil Tool, we'd have folded years ago."

Lisa's mind was working again like an efficient secretary. "Was the helicopter insured?"

"Of course. Herb couldn't have got the loan to buy it otherwise. But that's the trouble: he had to go in hock for every move he made. The bank owned everything around the place, even the furniture. So Martha's still broke." He pounded the table. "Damn! I wish there was more I could do to help."

Lisa's mind was still clicking like a computer. "How about personal coverage? Did Herb have any life insurance?"

"Not much. It isn't easy to get it in this business. And it's certainly not cheap. Oh, I know there was a small GI policy, but that's about all. Again, it's a hell of a situation. I'm sure sorry about Bart Jeppsen, but I just wish whoever killed him had picked a time when he was alone."

"I see what you mean," I said. "Well, we can't bring either of them back, that's for sure. But maybe we can help find out who was behind it. Let's get out to that rig and try, anyway."

"I'm with you," Jack said. I paid the check and we drove the half mile back to Grundy Aviation.

As we approached the red-and-white Bell helicopter, Jack asked me if I'd like to take over the copilot's seat. "After all," he said, "a pilot never likes to ride in back when he can sit up front."

I grinned. "That's right. But not this time. I hate helicopters, anyway. So if you don't mind playing chauffeur, I'll crawl in back with Lisa." I knew she'd prefer it that way, too.

"Okay with me. Say, where did you learn to fly, Johnny?"

"Originally Dayton. Started while I was still in high school. But I got most of my hours in Viet Nam."

"Really? Same with me. Looks as if you and I have a few things in common." He grinned, too. "Just a couple of old fly-boys."

We boarded the helicopter, again that odd eggbeater sound whined above our heads, and once more we headed out over the Gulf of Mexico.

I still had no idea what we'd learn there.

15

THIS TIME, we were greeted by one of the roughnecks, a big, burly man I'd met briefly when Lieutenant Mendez had interviewed the crew several days earlier. His name, I remembered, was Tom Ledbetter.

"Hello there, Mr. McCoy," he said. As he spoke, the three open spaces where he once had teeth were plainly visible. "What brings you out here today?"

"Same thing," I said. "We're still trying to find out how that chopper got blown up the other night. Is Charlie Delman here?"

"No, but Paul's down below. I can wake him up if it's important."

"Wake him up? At this time of day?"

"You haven't been around the oil patch much, have you?" Ledbetter said with some scorn.

"Johnny's only been in town for a few days," Jack interjected hastily. He turned to me. "This is a twenty-four-hour-a-day business," he explained. "Seven days a week. So everyone gets his shut-eye when he can."

"Oh, I see. Anyway," I asked the rig hand, "who's Paul?"

"Paul Duval. He's the new superintendent Calco

Oil sent over yesterday. He's taken Charlie Delman's place.''

"You mean Charlie is off for a few days?"

"Not off. Out. I hear he quit the company."

"Really? Any idea why?"

The roughneck shrugged. "Who knows? It happens all the time. Maybe he got a better offer."

"From whom, I wonder."

"Damned if I know. Why don't you ask Paul?"

"We hate to wake the poor man up," Lisa put in.

"Oh, that's okay. He's had at least three hours. Come with me."

We followed Tom Ledbetter down a short flight of steps to the crew's Spartan quarters below. With its plain iron beds and occasional straight-back chairs, the room looked almost like a prison cell without the bars. I'd heard that oilfield hands make good money, but decided again that the PR business was more to my liking.

Paul Duval was lying on one of the beds, fully clothed. Obviously accustomed to having his sleep interrupted at any time, he wakened almost instantly. Ledbetter introduced us and immediately went back topside.

Duval was a wiry little man with an olive complexion and straight black hair. "Excuse me a minute. I'll be right with you." He spoke with a trace of an accent—almost French, but not quite— which Lisa later explained was typical of Cajuns from southern Louisiana.

He stepped into the small cubicle at the end of the room and reappeared a few moments later, drying his hands and face with a small towel. He sat down in one of the chairs and motioned the rest of us into others. "Now," he said, "what can I do for you?"

"Well, frankly," I began, "we're trying to help find out who killed Bart Jeppsen."

"Afraid I can't help you with that, much as I'd like to. He was my friend, too, you know. But I was nowhere near this rig the night it happened."

"I know. That's why we were really looking for Charlie Delman. He was the last person to talk to Bart before the chopper took off. He even helped put the box aboard—the box we think contained the bomb."

"Good God! You certainly don't think Charlie had anything to do with it, do you? He and Bart had been friends for years!"

"I know that, Mr. Duval," I said.

"Paul."

"Paul. And, no we don't think Charlie himself was involved. But somebody was, and we were hoping he could give us a hint—some clue that might point to who that somebody is."

"Have you talked to the rig hands?"

"Yes, or at least I was here when Lieutenant Mendez interviewed them individually. They all denied having anything to do with it—or knowing anything about it."

Duval held up his hands. "Then I don't see what you'll gain by going through the whole procedure again."

I sighed. "I guess you're right. But can you at least show me what the box looked like?"

"Afraid I can't do that either. There are a bunch of bits upstairs—some in their original cartons—and you're welcome to look at them if you want.

But according to the news reports, this was a special box that Bart had brought out here with him, with compartments for bit records and other small items. They must have more of 'em back at the Jeppsen plant.''

I blew out a breath. ''So I guess we're back to square one. Well, thanks anyway, Paul.'' I got up to go, and Lisa and Jack followed suit. ''Just one other thing. Do you know where Charlie's working now?''

''No, I don't. But I hear he got a hell of an offer from somebody. The word'll get out in a couple of days, I'm sure.''

''Okay, thanks again.''

Lisa and Jack preceded me up the short flight of stairs to the octagonal-shaped pad above. I was just about to step up behind them when I heard Paul Duval turn on the radio. The only sound was a loud squeal, followed by Paul's equally loud voice. ''Damn this thing!'' he shouted.

Just on a strange hunch—I don't know why—I stepped back into the room. ''What's with the radio?'' I asked.

''Oh, this bastard thing goes on the blink every time you look at it. That's one thing the men will sure miss about Charlie. They tell me he was the only one who could keep it working right.''

''Oh? Really?''

''Yeah, they say he had a way with such things. Same with the electric can opener when it went on the fritz a while back. I guess when it comes to electricity, some guys have it and some don't.''

I waved goodbye. ''You've been a big help, Paul.''

THAT EVENING, Lisa invited me to dinner at her apartment. "How about a home-cooked meal for a change?" she asked as we pulled up to her Montrose Avenue apartment building. "I broil a mean steak."

"Sounds great," I said. And it did.

Once again, she mixed Scotches in her small kitchen and then plumped herself down on the white sofa with her long legs tucked underneath. We sipped our drinks slowly, at first in total silence.

Then she reached out her hand to mine. "I've got to tell you something, Johnny. I owe you that."

"You don't owe me anything, Lisa."

"Okay, then maybe I just want to."

"What?"

"I've never been a girl who sleeps around. I guess you know that by now."

"Please, Lisa, you don't have to . . . ."

"No, wait. Let me finish. During all the years since I met Bart, there's never been anyone else for me. I mean anyone."

"I know that, Lisa. Whatever you and Bart had, it must have been something special."

"It was, Johnny. Really special. And it won't be easy to get over it. I knew that when I made the big decision to break it off. But when I do . . . ."

She leaned toward me and I leaned toward her from the other end of the sofa. We met in the middle. Her lips were cool, then warm, then almost demanding. I finally broke our embrace.

"Now let me tell *you* something, Lisa. Believe me, I understand how you feel. And I won't push you. But whenever you want to, I'll be ready.''

She laughed. "I just bet you will."

I laughed, too. "Right now I'm ready to think about dinner. That *is* why you invited me here, isn't it?''

"Right! I'll go put on the steak, and you can mix us another drink."

During dinner, we talked about a lot of things. But uppermost in our minds—other than the understanding we had reached earlier—was the unsolved murder.

"That Charlie Delman certainly had the opportunity," she pointed out.

"Yes, he sure did. And from what Paul Duval said, he also would have known how to rig a bomb. But he still didn't have a motive."

"I wonder," Lisa said. "I just wonder."

As it turned out, we wouldn't have to wait long to find the answer to that one.

16

WHEN I ARRIVED at the Jeppsen plant at eight
o'clock Monday morning, there were several
things I wanted to discuss with Roger Lathrop—
most importantly, the forthcoming sales managers' meeting. Time was drawing near.

But the door to Roger's office was closed. Apparently he was busy with something else.

"Guess who's in there," Lisa said.

"Who?"

"Charlie Delman."

"No! Really?"

"That's right. Maybe your hunch last night
wasn't all wrong."

"It was your hunch, too, remember? I wonder
what's going on."

"I guess we'll find out soon enough. Meanwhile,
I'm having trouble finding a place to hold that
sales meeting you were talking about. I've
checked with all the spots we usually use—The
Woodlands, Columbia Lakes and the rest. They're
all booked up. We're not giving them much notice,
you know."

"Well, keep trying, Lisa. There's got to be someplace we can get in."

Just then the phone rang on Lisa's desk. "Hello,

Lisa Wallace,'' she said. There was a short pause.
"Yes, I did call you the other day.... That's right,
about thirty people.... Really? Hey, that's super.
We'll take it.... Yes, arrival Friday evening,
departure on Sunday.... Absolutely. I'll get a
deposit in the mail today without fail.... Great!
Thanks so much.''

As Lisa hung up the phone, she grinned at me triumphantly. "We got it! Lakeway had a last-minute
cancellation, today, so we're in like Flynn.''

"Where's Lakeway?''

"On Lake Travis, about twenty-five miles west
of Austin. It's really a super place for a meeting.
We couldn't have done better.''

As always, my mind reverted to my favorite
form of transportation. "They have an airstrip
there?''

"Yes, as a matter of fact they do. Right on the
property.''

"Then it's got to be a good place!'' I paused.
"Say, Lisa, how about flying up there with me on
Friday?''

"I think I'd like that, Johnny.'' Once more her
eyes held a promise. "I think I'd like that a lot.''

We were busy discussing more of the details of
the meeting when the door to Roger Lathrop's office opened, and Roger and Charlie Delman
stepped out with their arms around each other's
shoulders. They looked like two fraternity
brothers meeting at a twenty-fifth reunion.

"Hello, Johnny,'' Roger said. "Greet our new
Vice-President of Engineering!''

So that's why Delman left Calco Oil, I thought.
But all I said was, "Congratulations, Charlie.''

"Yes, this calls for another press release," Lathrop went on. "It's a hell of a thing that made it possible, but it's the best news around here since Bart's tragic death last Wednesday evening."

Delman's leathery face split into a broad grin. "That's mighty kind of you, Roger."

"And you know I mean it," Roger said. He turned to me. "Fact is, Johnny, we've wanted a man of Charlie's caliber on the staff for a long time. Never had a job open that was big enough for him. Now, with Bart gone, we do. And, let's face it, I'm just a numbers man myself." He turned back to Delman. "I don't have to tell you how much your technical expertise is going to mean to us, Charlie. You're stepping into an important job, but I know we can count on you."

Again, Charlie grinned his appreciation.

During the next hour, we all collaborated on planning the agenda for the sales meeting at Lakeway. Then, after that was buttoned up, I went back to my borrowed office to draft the release announcing Charlie Delman's appointment to his new post at Jeppsen Oil Tool.

I handed it to Lisa and asked her to type it up and send it out to the news media. Then I suddenly remembered I had another press contact I wanted to make—Howard Ketchum, who'd written the exposé I'd seen in the Sunday *Post*.

I dialed the *Post* and, after a short delay, was put through to the reporter's desk. "Hello, Howard Ketchum." A clacking of typewriters sounded in the background.

"My name's Johnny McCoy," I began. "I'm in

town for a while, doing some PR work for Jeppsen Oil Tool.''

"I'm sure that's an important job, Mr. McCoy," Ketchum said. "But it's a little out of my line. Maybe you should talk with our business editor.''

"No, thanks. Right now I need to talk with you. It's about your article in yesterday's paper, the one covering Houston's porno industry.''

"Oh, that! Yours isn't the first call that's come in about it. But what's it got to do with Jeppsen Oil Tool?''

"I don't know. That's what I'm trying to find out. Maybe you can help.''

"I don't see how. After all. . . .''

"Look," I interrupted. "The fact is that you might be able to blow this whole thing wide open. And maybe I can help you at the same time." I looked at my watch. "Are you free for lunch today?''

There was a moment's pause. "Yes. I guess so. Do you know where our place is?''

"No, but I can find out in a hurry.''

"Okay. Then pick me up in front of the building at 11:45. I'll be wearing a blue-and-white checked sport coat.''

"Great! I'll be in a gold Cutlass. See you then. And thanks a lot." I broke the connection.

"SO THAT'S ABOUT ALL I KNOW," Ketchum was saying. "As I pointed out in that article, there seems to be more porno businesses in Houston these days than anywhere else in the country, and most of it is controlled by people from the outside. A lot of us here don't like it." He was a thin-faced young

man with a well-trimmed beard that was thicker
than the blond hair that barely covered his ruddy
scalp. I judged him to be in his late twenties.

We had finished lunch at Mark's, a warm,
friendly restaurant off the Southwest Freeway at
Hillcroft, and were now sipping our coffee.

"And you think Marty Angel may be the top
man," I said.

"That's right." Ketchum drew on his pipe.
"But, of course, I can't be sure."

"Then, what's next?"

"For the porno industry? Probably just more of
the same. Let's face it, there is a market for all
that stuff, and the police can't, or won't, lift a
finger to stop it."

"How about you? Do you honestly think *you* can
do anything about it?"

Ketchum paused while he relit his pipe.
"Probably not. But at least I'm trying. That piece
you read yesterday won't be the last, I can assure
you. I'll keep digging—and reporting what I un-
cover."

"Doesn't that put you in jeopardy, too? I mean,
Marty Angel and his cronies obviously have to
know you're after them. As a reporter, you're not
exactly invisible, you know."

"Yes, I do know. And, sure, I've thought about
it. But, well, somebody's got to take a stand.
Anyway, Johnny, you still haven't told me why
you're so concerned about all this."

He was right. I hadn't. But then I began to
realize how important Howard Ketchum's help
might be. It could be a mistake to hold out on him.
He was being open and sincere with me, and I felt

I'd better respond in kind. So I told him about my visit to the Wahoo Lounge on Friday night—*all* about it—including the telephone conversation I'd overheard before leaving.

Ketchum whistled. "That *does* put Randy Jeppsen in a hole, doesn't it? Now I can see why you wanted to talk about it. I wonder how much money is involved, and what it's owed for."

"I have no idea. There's another question, too. Where did Randy get the bankroll to open the Wahoo Lounge in the first place."

"Hard to tell. Maybe he got a loan from Marty Angel." He snapped his fingers. "Maybe that's why Randy owes him that money."

I thought for a moment, then shook my head. "I kind of doubt that. His girl friend—or one of them, anyway—told me he's had the place for a couple of years. Does that sound about right?"

"Yes, I think it's been open about that long." He paused briefly. "Oh, I see what you mean. A man like Marty Angel wouldn't wait two years to collect on a debt."

"Right. And another thing. He probably wouldn't have loaned money to Randy at that time, anyway. Perhaps now, but not then. From what everybody tells me—and what I've seen for myself, too, for that matter—Randy's never had a regular job or anything else to give him much of a credit rating. As far as I can tell, the Wahoo Lounge is the only business enterprise of any kind he's ever been involved with."

"God! Really? How old is he?"

"I'm not sure. Probably about the same age his dad was when he started Jeppsen Oil Tool." I realized again what an enormous difference there was between father and son. "Anyway, he must be close to thirty."

"Jesus! I'm twenty-eight, and I've been at the *Post* almost seven years. And before that I worked my way through the University of Houston. I wonder what it must be like not to have to work for a living."

I grinned. "I don't know. Never had the experience. But if Randy Jeppsen is an example of the result, I don't think I want to."

"Well, how *has* he lived all these years?"

I shrugged. "Worthlessly. Apparently, he's been getting handouts from the family—mainly from his mother—and I guess they've been pretty sizable."

"There's your answer, then, Johnny. That must explain how he was able to open the Wahoo Lounge. After all, it doesn't take much to start a deal like that. Look at one of those places in the daytime and it's a dump."

"I guess you're right. It's not exactly the Petroleum Club in the evening, either. Anyway, let's get back to Randy's debt to Marty Angel. And even more significantly, what Angel will do if it isn't paid back pronto."

Ketchum winced. "From what I hear, that could be anything."

"What do you really know about Marty Angel's background, Howard? Has he ever actually killed anybody?"

He shrugged. "That's hard to say. Anyway, it wouldn't surprise me to learn that he's *had* people killed."

"And, knowing that, you're still pursuing it?"

He grinned. "And, knowing that, *you're* still pursuing it?"

I grinned back. "I guess we're both crazy." I paid the check and we both left.

As I dropped Howard Ketchum off in front of the *Houston Post*'s castlelike building on the Southwest Freeway, he handed me his card. "Thanks for the lunch," he said. "Call me anytime if I can help. My home number's on the back." He started to leave, then turned and put his hands on the side of the car. "But I'll tell you one thing."

"What's that?"

"If you really want to get a line on Marty Angel's past, you won't find it in Houston. That story has got to be in Chicago."

"Thanks again, Howard. I'll remember that."

As I drove back to the Jeppsen plant, I thought about what Howard Ketchum had told me. I didn't have any idea how to track down information in Chicago.

But I knew who would.

17

As soon as I got back to the Jeppsen plant, I immediately put a long-distance call through to Buzzy Branigan. As New York's number-one celebrity columnist and man-about-town, Buzzy knew just about everything worth knowing. And as an old and close friend, I was sure he'd help me all he could. He always has.

I was lucky to find him in his office. "Hello, Johnny," his voice boomed over the wire. "How are things in Houston?"

"Fine—well, pretty good. How did you know I was here?"

"I didn't. That is, not until a couple of hours ago. Your gal Marsha called and told me you're mixed up in another murder mystery."

"That's right. Bart Jeppsen." I quickly gave Buzzy a rundown on the case.

"Sounds like you've got yourself into a real hornet's nest. But how can I help you, old friend?"

"You probably can't—with the murder, that is. But there's another side to it that's got me stumped." I went on to explain Randy Jeppsen's apparent involvement with Marty Angel. "Anyway," I concluded, "Angel may hold the key to the whole mishmash. What do you know about him?"

"Not much. I've never heard of him around the Big City. From Chicago, isn't he?"

"Exactly. So now the question is: who do you know there that might be able to give me a line on the guy? Chicago's new territory to me."

"That's easy. Sid Markowitz."

"Who?"

Branigan chuckled. "I can see you *don't* know Chicago, do you? Sid Markowitz. Does a column for the *Tribune* something like mine here in New York. He's also got a daytime TV show, called 'On Your Mark.' You know, interviews, showbiz personalities, local political issues, that sort of thing."

"Sounds like just the man I'm looking for."

"Well, at least it'd be a good start."

"Is Markowitz a friend of yours?"

That was almost a rhetorical question, and Branigan's answer came as no surprise. "Christ, yes. We've known each other for years. Tell him I suggested you call him."

"Thanks a million, Buzzy. I'll sure do that."

"Glad to help. Take care!"

My next call, of course, was to Sid Markowitz. When I told his secretary that Buzzy Branigan had referred me, she put me right through.

"Hello, Mr. Markowitz?" I began. "My name's Johnny McCoy, and Buzzy Branigan suggested you might be able to help me with a problem."

The recommendation was clearly an Open Sesame. "Buzzy Branigan! God, I haven't seen him in a coon's age! How is the old rascal, anyway?"

"Same as ever. And he says you know Chicago about as well as he does New York."

"Could be. We're both in the same racket. What's your problem?"

I decided to use the direct approach. "Marty Angel. I'm trying to get a line on him."

At the mention of Angel's name, some of the cordiality disappeared and Markowitz's voice took on a note of caution. "Well, now, that may not be so easy. Who did you say you were?"

"Johnny McCoy. I'm in the PR business. I'm based in New York, but right now I'm in Houston doing some work for Jeppsen Oil Tool."

"Oh, yes, Bart Jeppsen. That was an awful thing, wasn't it? But you still haven't told me what you want with Marty Angel."

Once again, as briefly as I could, I described Randy Jeppsen's probable connection with Marty Angel, and why Angel might be involved some-how with Bart's murder.

Some of Markowitz's warmth returned. "I see. That does put you in a box, doesn't it?"

"Sure does. Is there any way you can help get me out of it?"

"Well, I'll say this. Yes, I do know a few things about Mr. Angel, and some of them aren't very pretty. But I frankly don't think I'd better discuss them over the phone. I hope you understand what I'm saying."

"I do indeed, Mr. Markowitz. And what you're saying makes me all the more anxious to talk with you about it. How about if I came to Chicago?"

"By all means, that would be better. Lots better."

He'd given me an opening, and I took it. "Fine! Suppose I fly up there this evening. Would you have time to see me sometime tomorrow?"

Markowitz paused for a moment. "I guess that'd be all right. Tell you what. . . I've got a taping of my TV show tomorrow morning at eleven. If you want to stop by the studio at eleven-thirty, we could have lunch together and you could still catch a late afternoon flight back."

"That's perfect! I really appreciate it."

"No problem. Who knows. . . maybe you can help me, too." He told me how to get to the TV studio, and we hung up.

As you've gathered, I hate going places without my Bonanza. When you own an airplane, you don't enjoy leaving it on the ground. But there are times, admittedly, when the airlines come in handy. This was one of those times.

I gave Lisa the job of making my reservations, and then dialed my office in New York. Marsha Henley, my person Friday, sounded worried.

"Hey, Boss," she said immediately, "can't you ever stick to PR and stay out of murder cases?" She'd obviously been reading the papers. "Why do you always get mixed up in these things, anyway?"

I grinned. "Just lucky, I guess. What's new at the office?"

"Nothing that can't wait. But for God's sake, tell me what's going on in Houston."

Once more, I went over the essential facts of the case. I was beginning to feel like a TV announcer reciting a news break and for all three networks.

"Well, be careful, will you? That Irish luck of yours can't last forever."

"It has so far. Anyway, Marsha, if you need me, I'll be in Chicago tomorrow."

"Chicago! One does get around, doesn't one! For heaven's sake, why Chicago? I didn't know they had oil wells in Lake Michigan."

"They don't. But I need to check something out there." I didn't see any reason to give her more of the details, so I simply told her where I'd be staying and left it at that.

Marsha's parting shot was, "Okay. But please take it easy. After all, I don't know where else I could get a job that would keep me this poor."

I laughed and we hung up.

Lisa had got me on an early dinner flight, so after checking out with Roger, I drove back to the Shamrock to pack a bag and headed north toward Houston's Intercontinental Airport. I pulled into the "Park and Fly" parking lot, rode the courtesy van to the terminal and boarded the airplane. Two Scotches and a steak later, I was in Chicago.

As I say, sometimes the airlines perform absolute miracles. The thousand miles from Houston to Chicago takes just a flat two hours. As I checked into my hotel, I was thinking, now, if only some genius could figure out a way to travel the twenty miles from O'Hare to the Loop in *one* hour, we would indeed be living in a wondrous age.

18

I GOT TO THE TV STATION just as Sid Markowitz was
concluding his interview with a young rock star
who was appearing in the area. I was greeted by a
frosty receptionist with an English accent, who
ushered me into a small auditorium adjacent to the
studio. Through the window, I could see a small,
rotund man with a frizz of white hair that sat like
a halo around his otherwise bald scalp. His eyes
looked like an owl's.

As Markowitz ended the interview, his off-
camera announcer spoke into a mike. "Be with us
again tomorrow," he said, "and meet another
headline figure 'On Your Mark'!" The floodlights
dimmed, and Sid Markowitz came out into the
auditorium.

I rose to greet him. "It's darn nice of you to see
me on such short notice, Mr. Markowitz."

"Glad to do it. Any friend of Buzzy Branigan's
can't be all bad. Are you ready for lunch? If we go
now we'll beat the rush."

"Fine with me," I said. "Lead the way."

Markowitz took me to a sort of English pub
around the corner. As he'd predicted, the place
was still half empty, but all those present seemed
to recognize him with pleasure. I could see that Sid

Markowitz was indeed the Chicago counterpart of Buzzy Branigan.

"Well, now," he said as we sat down, "tell me more about yourself." He was obviously a man accustomed to gaining information as well as dispensing it.

Once again I told him a little of my own background, particularly stressing the events of the past week.

As the waiter finished taking our orders, Markowitz said, "I think maybe I *can* help you, Johnny. But we've got to get one thing straight first."

"You're calling the shots, Sid."

"Okay. The fact is that I do have some information about Marty Angel, and I may have more any day now. I'm not sure exactly when; that's the nature of this business. But I'm not ready to divulge it all—not yet. At least not publicly. I'm talking to you because you're a friend of Buzzy's—you might as well know I verified that after you called me yesterday. So whatever I tell you—for now, anyway—has to be kept confidential. Is that understood?"

"Absolutely."

The waiter brought our soup at that moment, and Markowitz waited until he was out of earshot before continuing. "All right. Marty Angel is the biggest, lousiest crook that's been around Chicago since Al Capone. It's common knowledge that he's got his fingers in gambling, prostitution and a half dozen other rackets, and it's thought that he also controls most of the dope trade in the Midwest as well. But that part's never been proved. The cops have been trying for years. Somehow, Mr. Angel always seems to stay one jump ahead of 'em."

"Sounds like something out of an old Edward G. Robinson movie."

The waiter brought our lamb chops, and Markowitz paused again. Then he went on. "That's exactly what it is. Maybe worse."

"I don't know how to ask this, but . . . well, have *you* been involved with Marty Angel in any way?"

Markowitz's owlish eyes looked at me sharply. "That's precisely why this has to remain confidential, Johnny. The fact is that I've been on Marty Angel's trail for years. And he knows it—or at least suspects it, I'm sure of that. And I just may be getting close to the end." He pointed a finger at me as he continued, still in low tones with increased intensity. "Look, a guy in my business gets a lot of privileges—that's obvious. But with those privileges goes a certain responsibility. If I can somehow get the goods on Marty Angel, it'll be the best thing I've ever done."

He leaned back, seemingly relieved to have gotten that off his chest. For, like Howard Ketchum, Sid Markowitz clearly took his job with utmost seriousness and dedication. Then he dropped the real bombshell.

"But all that is only one reason I'm going to nail that sonofabitch. The other reason is personal, deeply personal." He jabbed his knife into a lamb chop, almost cleaving it in half. "Fact is, my kid sister, Ida, had a daughter who got hooked on drugs while she was still in junior high. It broke up the whole family and brought on a divorce. Ida nearly had a complete mental breakdown. And then, to top it all off, the kid finally—just last year—jumped out of an eleventh-story window of the fleabag hotel she was living in at the time.'' The man was openly crying now. "Can you believe that? A nice kid, from a good family, a suicide at sixteen!''

I hardly knew what to say. "Jesus, Sid. That's a hell of a blow. And you think Marty Angel was responsible.''

"I *know* it!'' he almost shouted. Then, with an obvious effort, he brought himself under control. "Oh, there was no proof. There never is in those cases. The police just threw up their hands. But Angel is the kingpin behind it all, I'm sure of that. And *that*, Johnny, is why I'll never be satisfied until the bastard gets what's coming to him.''

"I'm with you, Sid. I'll sure do what I can. And you can still be a big help. For instance, what do you know bout Marty Angel's activities in Houston?''

Markowitz shook his head. "Now that's something I can't help you with. I didn't even know he was operating there until you told me. But I'll say this: whatever he's doing there, he's up to no good. And if Bart Jeppsen's son—what's his name, Randy—is mixed up with Marty Angel, he's in trouble, too. Bad trouble.''

"I'm afraid Randy is involved with him, Sid. Deeply involved.'' I reminded him about the phone call I'd overheard in the Wahoo Lounge. "After all, that's why I'm here. As I see it, it's a perfect motive for Randy to have killed his father.''

Markowitz sat silently for a moment. His fingertips drummed a rhythm on the table. Then he smiled grimly. "You know, from what you say, there's another possibility, too.''

"What's that?"

"Well, let's say Randy owes Marty Angel a lot of money—a gambling debt or whatever. Then let's say his family turned off the faucet and refused to keep bank-rolling him."

"You've got it. That's exactly the picture."

"Okay. Now let's say our friend Randy wanted to do away with his old man, but didn't have the guts. I've known a lot of young punks like that, and they're all pretty much the same."

"What are you leading up to, Sid?"

"Just this. Suppose Marty Angel knew all this— which he probably does—so he killed Bart Jepp- sen, or had him killed, because that way Randy would come into money to pay off the debt. How about that? Isn't it possible?"

I slammed my fist on the table. "By God, Sid, that all fits perfectly! Jesus, I never thought of it that way! Now I've *got* to keep after it."

Markowitz stared up at me. "You look as if you could handle yourself in a fight, Johnny. But not against knives and guns. So watch your step, fella. As I say, Marty Angel doesn't exactly play by the rules."

We finished our lunch. I picked up the tab, and we started to leave.

"Oh, one more thing, Sid. I forgot to ask you what Marty Angel looks like."

"I thought you'd want to know that." Marko- witz reached in his inside breast pocket and with- drew a smudged newspaper clipping with a single photo. He handed it to me across the table. "That's him. Not hard to recognize once you've seen him."

Marty Angel didn't look as if he'd be easy to forget. He was a squat-looking man with a block of a head that seemed to grow right out of his shoulders. There was no neck at all, just that square head glued to his shoulders. His eyes looked as if they could fire bullets.

I thanked Markowitz again, caught a cab back to O'Hare and boarded the afternoon flight to Houston.

Throughout the two-hour trip I kept looking at that square head with the gun-barrel eyes. Somehow, on this trip, the two Scotches did nothing to calm my nerves.

19

I PROMISED TO CALL LISA as soon as the plane landed, so I stopped by one of the pay phones in Houston's ultramodern terminal and dialed her number. As usual, she answered after the first ring.

"Hi! How did you make out with Sid Markowitz?"

"Fine. He was a big help." I briefly filled her in on the details.

"How about picking me up for dinner? It's about that time, and I could sure go for more of Pierre's French cooking."

"Good idea. I'll be there as soon as the traffic'll let me."

I hung up, slung my garment bag over my shoulder and rode the "Park and Fly" van back to my car. An hour and a half later, Lisa and I were back at Pierre's. Again, the food equalled the hospitality. And once more she used the back of the menu as a notepad.

"So our list of suspects keeps growing," she said. "Before we had Cynthia, Randy, Laurie and Roger. Now we add Charlie Delman."

"Oh, come on, Lisa! Sure, he had the opportunity—more so than anybody else. And, yes, I know he ended up with a vice-presidency at Jepp-sen Oil Tool. But I still don't see that as a motive for murder."

Lisa put down her knife and fork and looked at me directly. "Oh, no? He got a lot more than a plain vice-presidency, that's for sure."

"How do you mean?"

"He's practically taken Bart's place in the company, that's what I mean. Roger's the boss now, no question about that. But get this . . . while you were in Chicago today, Roger had me type up a buy-sell agreement between them—the same kind of deal he had with Bart. The lawyers still have to go over it, of course, but that's just a formality. So good old Charlie Delman is now the heir apparent to the whole shebang. You don't call that a motive?"

"Good God, Lisa, I see what you're getting at. This is still all supposition, of course, but if Charlie did kill Bart, that makes Roger the next target."

"Exactly. And I think we ought to warn him about it."

"Can't do that, Lisa. We're still just guessing, remember? Besides, there's always the possibility that Roger and Charlie cooked the whole deal up together. I know the oil patch is a friendly business—everybody keeps telling me that—but those two looked almost too chummy when they came out of Roger's office yesterday morning. So I think we've just got to play it cool, at least until we have more to go on."

Lisa took a sip of wine. "Let's change the subject. Tell me more about Sid Markowitz."

"A very sincere guy, Lisa. I liked him. And he

came up with a brand new slant we hadn't even thought of." I went on to tell her about Sid's suggestion that maybe Marty Angel was behind the whole affair, that perhaps *he* had arranged Bart's murder as the only way to get his payoff from Randy.

Lisa made a note on the back of the menu. "So that gives us still another prime suspect."

"Right. And to look at him, I'd say he wouldn't mind killing his best friend." I showed her the photo of Angel that I'd gotten from Sid Markowitz.

Lisa took one look at it and shivered involuntarily. "Jesus, that face is enough to scare a gorilla."

I shrugged. "I know what you mean. But there's only one way to find out more about the case, and that's to keep digging." I'm sure I sounded more casual than I felt. "Anyway, after I drop you off at your apartment, I'm going to pay another visit to the Wahoo Lounge."

Lisa reached her hand across the table to mine. Her eyes were misty. "Look, Johnny, somehow I feel we're in this thing together. If you have to go back to that place, I want to go with you."

My voice rose. "Absolutely not!" I squeezed her hand and then said in a much softer tone, "I appreciate what you're saying, Lisa. Believe me, I do. And I'm beginning to feel the same way. But there's no way I'm going to let you get that involved."

We finished our meal in silence. I paid the check, drove Lisa back to her apartment and went out to the sleazy shopping center at Richmond and Gessner.

Again, the Wahoo Lounge was bathed in garish

lights; again, I paid the ten-dollar admission fee
and the additional ten for a watered-down double
Scotch; again, the scene of blatant prostitution
permeated the sordid atmosphere all around.

But this time, along with the motley array of
sweaty customers, there was a new face in the
crowd. A squat, square-headed man was just
emerging from the narrow hallway behind the bar.
I didn't need a formal introduction to know who it
was.

I figured that the direct approach was as good as
any. "Mr. Angel? My name's Johnny McCoy. Can I
talk to you for a minute?"

Those gun-barrel eyes turned in my direction.
Somehow, I had the feeling that they could see
what was directly behind me. "About what?" He
said it with no inflection, almost without interest.

"About Randy Jeppsen. I'm a friend of the family."

"Oh, you are, are you?" He still didn't seem to
give a damn one way or the other.

"Yes. I understand Randy owes you some
money."

Angel's expression didn't change, but for the
first time he seemed to be aware of my presence. I
could sense I'd at least touched a nerve. "Let's
talk in the back."

He led me down the hall to the tiny office of the
Wahoo Lounge. It was empty. Angel closed the
door, sat down behind the card table and motioned me into the other chair. "Now," he said, spit-
ting out the words. "You say you understand
Randy owes me some money."

"That's right. At least, that's what I hear. So my

question, Mr. Angel, is why? What does he owe
you the money for?''

"What's it to you?''

"How much is the loan, Mr. Angel?''

"You haven't answered my question—what's it
to you?''

I never was able to do a very good Humphrey
Bogart imitation, but I figured I had to hold my
ground. "And you still haven't answered *my* question. How much does he owe you and why?''

"Just like that, huh?''

I shrugged. "They're simple questions.''

"Okay, McCoy, here's your answer.'' For the
first time, he put emphasis into his words. "None
of your fucking business.''

I'll admit I was beginning to get a queasy feeling
in the pit of my stomach, but I was determined not
to show it. "That's not an acceptable answer.'' If I
thought I was going to scare *him*, I was *really*
kidding myself.

"Okay, then let me answer it like this.'' He
rapped on the wall beside him, and the door
opened immediately.

The opening was filled—both top to bottom and
side to side—by an enormous goon of a man with a
twisted grin. He looked like TV's Incredible Hulk.
"Hello, Marty,'' he said. "You called for me?''

"Yes, Boris,'' Angel said. "Mr. McCoy here apparently has had enough to drink for the evening,
so he's leaving now.'' Again he spat out the words
without emotion. "If he has any trouble finding
the exit, help him out, please.''

There's obviously a time to stop playing Humphrey Bogart, and this was one of those times. I

left without further urging. Driving back to the Shamrock, I somehow had trouble holding the wheel steady. It wasn't the Scotch.

As usual, I parked in the Shamrock garage and started to walk the half block to the hotel entrance. I thought a short walk might do me good, anyway. I was wrong.

Halfway through the Shamrock's tailored grounds, just as I was approaching the entrance to Trader Vic's, a soft voice behind me said, "Hey, buddy, got a match?".

I turned and got a glimpse of Boris's twisted grin. As he swung his huge fist, a sledgehammer exploded in my gut. I fought back the pain, took a gulp of air, and then remembering my marine training, I aimed my knee at the lower part of Boris's anatomy.

But just at that moment I caught a glimpse of something else coming at me from the other side. That was all I remembered.

As Sid Markowitz had suggested, I'm usually pretty handy in a fight. But not against the likes of Boris. Not when he's got another goon with him, and especially not when the other goon is armed with a lead pipe.

20

I FINALLY AWOKE in a state of utter confusion. I was puzzled. I couldn't decide where I was. On the one hand, I was surrounded by soft, lush greenery, and there was a delightfully sweet smell of flowers all around. Aha, I thought, I made it: I'm in heaven!

But then I noticed a hard pounding on the side of my left temple. It wasn't just a throb; it was a deep, searing pain. My whole head felt like a sidewalk being dug up by a pneumatic drill. No, I thought then, this can't be heaven. Oh, well, at least I'm among old friends.

Some minutes later, a measure of consciousness came back and I sat up. The tan facade of the Shamrock came into view and the puzzle was solved. I'd been lying in the bushes to the side of the hotel. Then I remembered Boris and his crony with the lead pipe. I looked at my watch: it read 6:15. I finally made it to my feet and managed to wobble to the hotel entrance. The doorman, obviously accustomed to having drunks stagger in at dawn, didn't say a word.

Back in my room, I stripped and stepped into the shower. Five minutes later, as I toweled myself dry, the full impact of the incident hit me at last. It wasn't pleasant to contemplate.

Once before, while investigating the Chip Lloyd case in New York, I'd been zapped on the back of the head in my apartment. But that time the assailant remained hidden and his identity was unknown. So, in that sense, it had not been a direct act of vengeance.

This time it was decidedly different. The man who slugged me was Boris. The lead pipe was wielded by Boris's accomplice. They both worked for Marty Angel. And, from all reports, Mr. Angel had something to hide.

Exactly what that something was, I had no way of knowing. Neither Howard Ketchum nor Sid Markowitz had given me any hard facts—only suspicions, and even they were pretty vague. Certainly, Marty Angel himself had told me nothing whatsoever. But maybe he *thought* I knew, or might find out something solid.

In any case, the message was distinct and direct: lay off. I heard it loud and clear.

But I wasn't about to heed it.

I was reminded of the many times I'd gotten into bad weather in the Bonanza. Often, there'd been a strong temptation to make a 180-degree turn and head back in the opposite direction, which is precisely what the textbooks advise doing. And, admittedly, on a few occasions I'd set down at a nearby airport and waited until the storm passed over before continuing the flight. But usually, right or wrong, I pressed on. Maybe that's why some of my girl friends over the years have acquired a strong dislike for flying. So be it.

In this case, I thought perhaps a "copilot" might be helpful. Lieutenant Mendez had made it plain

that he didn't want my cooperation on the case.
But now I wanted his. After Marty Angel's clear
warning, I decided I'd be a damn fool not to.

I called Lisa's apartment. Again, she answered
promptly. "Hello?"

"Hi, Lisa, it's me."

"I've been thinking about you, Johnny. How did
things go last night at the Wahoo Lounge?"

"Okay. I saw Marty Angel." I decided not to
elaborate on the details. "Will you tell Roger I'll be
a little late today? It might be around lunchtime,
or even after."

She sounded surprised and a bit dismayed. "But
we've still got to finalize the details of the sales
meeting! And that's only a couple of days away!"

"I know, Lisa. We can get it all buttoned up this
afternoon."

"Is there something you're not telling me,
Johnny? Did something happen at the Wahoo
Lounge last night?"

"No. Well, not exactly. Honest, Lisa, it's nothing
to worry about. I'll tell you more about it when I
see you. Okay?"

She sighed. "Okay. But whatever's going on between you and Marty Angel, I feel that I'm responsible. I just wish I'd never asked you to get
involved in the first place."

"But I am involved, Lisa. And it's going to work
out all right, I promise. So don't worry."

"Okay, I'll try not to. See you later." She kissed
me through the wire and hung up.

An hour and a half later, I entered Lieutenant
Mendez's office at the police station on Riesner
Street. With clean clothes outside and breakfast

inside, I felt almost normal. The jackhammer at the side of my head was beginning to go away, but its mark hadn't.

"My God," Mendez said when he saw me. "What happened to you?"

I've always figured there's a time to play coy and a time to talk straight. This seemed to be one of the latter. "Lieutenant," I said, "I know you and I didn't exactly get off on the right foot together. I'm sorry about that, and if it was my fault I apologize. But right now I need your help, and I think maybe you could use mine."

He softened momentarily. "Okay, McCoy." He clasped his hands together on top of his metal desk and made a church steeple with his forefingers. "Tell me about it."

So I did—the whole story of my visits to the Wahoo Lounge, Randy's involvement with Marty Angel, my lunch with Howard Ketchum and, finally, the beating I'd taken at the hands of Angel's two goons. The only thing I withheld was my overnight trip to Chicago. Sid Markowitz had insisted that discussion should be kept confidential, and I respected his wishes.

Mendez had remained silent through all this. He just sat there doing little push-up exercises with his fingers. But when I finished he exploded.

"Jesus Christ, McCoy. I told you to let *us* handle the investigation." He spread his hands with exasperation. "Why in God's name didn't you listen to me?"

I did my best to remain calm. "Because I was already involved, even then. I'm not trying to step on your toes, Mendez, I'm just trying to help."

"So now I suppose you want a police escort every place you go!"

I could feel my Irish temper beginning to flare up again. "No, dammit! I just figured that two heads are better than one!"

My composure was gone; his had returned. Mendez fingered his mustache and said, "That, Mr. McCoy, depends on the two heads." He pointed at the bright red welt at my left temple. "The only thing that can be said for yours is that it's hard!" He eased his chair back and stood up. "Now, if you'll excuse me, I have work to do. If you're looking for further protection, you can always check the yellow pages under baby-sitters. You see, we have a saying for that. . . ."

"I know!" I cut him off. "You have a saying for that in Spanish. Translated it means: take your goddam smart-ass attitude and shove it!"

I don't usually drink during the day. This was one time I broke the rule.

21

I HAD TOLD LISA I wouldn't be in until around noon; I'd expected my visit with Mendez to last far longer than it did. As it was, still with no more information than I'd had before going downtown, I arrived at the Jeppsen plant just after ten.

"Well, well," Lisa said when I got off the elevator. "You're in early!" Then she noticed the side of my head. She ran from behind her desk and threw her arms around me. "Good heavens, Johnny! What happened?"

I didn't see any way out of it, so I told her, and then I narrated my brief encounter that morning in Mendez's office.

"Johnny, maybe he's right!" As I started to glare, she said, "No, wait a minute! I know you don't like the man. Neither do I, for that matter. But it *is* his job." Her eyes took on a thin veil of mist. "And if somebody else is going to get killed around here, please God let it be Lieutenant Mendez, not you!"

Obviously, Lisa had a point. There *was* danger involved, that was clear. But if that lead pipe had given me second thoughts—which it had—Mendez's attitude only served to spur me forward. But how to explain this to Lisa? I didn't know.

Just then the phone on Lisa's desk rang. She stepped over and picked up the receiver. "Mr. Lathrop's office.... Yes, he's here. Who may I say is calling...? Just a moment, please." She held the receiver away from her face. "It's for you, Johnny. Sid Markowitz."

I grabbed the receiver. "Hello, Sid. How are you?"

"I'm fine, Johnny. Where are you talking from?"

"Jeppsen Oil Tool, of course. Where did you think...."

"No, I mean *where*? It's important, Johnny!"

I caught the urgency in Sid's tone. "I'm right outside Roger Lathrop's office. Why?"

"Can you take it privately?"

"Of course." I told Lisa to transfer the call to my borrowed office. I ran back, closed the door and picked up the receiver. "Okay, Sid. Go ahead."

"You alone now?"

"Yes, Sid. Absolutely. Come on, what's up?"

"Remember I told you yesterday that I thought I was close to getting the goods on Marty Angel?"

I felt my pulse quicken. "Sure do, Sid. Has something new come up?"

"It has indeed. In spades."

"Tell me about it," I urged.

"I'm trying to! Last evening, one of Marty Angel's old hoods came by my apartment. Said he didn't dare go to the cops. Anyway, listen to this. He had books, records, photocopies of documents—the whole works—linking Angel to every illegal racket in Chicago. How about that!"

"And he turned over all that stuff to you?"

"He sure did. As I say, I guess he figured it'd be safer—for him, I mean—than turning it over to the police. If Angel found out, it'd be curtains for him. As it is, it's going to be curtains for Mr. Angel."

"How about *you*, Sid? You better watch your own step!"

"Oh, don't worry about me." He was actually chortling now. "I'm going to lock this stuff in a drawer here in my apartment, run over to the studio to tape the show and then come back and hustle it all down to the district attorney. Wait till you see the papers tomorrow!"

Just at that moment I heard a banging in the background, like something knocking on a door. Then the banging got louder.

"Sid! Sid!" I yelled. "Are you all right?"

"I think so, Johnny." But now he was no longer chortling.

The banging got still louder. Then I heard the sound of splintering wood.

"For God's sake, Sid, hang up and call the police."

And then a shot rang out. Just one single shot. Then a click and a dial tone. That was all.

I knew instantly that *I'd* see the papers the next day, but Sid Markowitz wouldn't.

Normally, my first instinct would have been to call the cops. But I had no connection with the Chicago Police Department, and even if I'd called them blindly, I couldn't have given them Sid's address. And after my bout with Lieutenant Mendez that morning, I certainly had no desire to call *him*.

There was one other obvious course of action. I dialed Sid's office in Chicago, got the frosty recep-

tionist and told her what had happened. All of it.
Now, with Sid dead, I saw no reason to withhold
any information—what little I had.

The receptionist gasped when I gave her the
news—she sounded as if she was about to faint—
but she assured me she'd relay the information to
the Chicago police and follow through as best she
could.

Personally, I felt utterly helpless. But there was
nothing more I could do.

The rest of the day was spent finalizing plans for
the Saturday sales meeting at Lakeway. It was
agreed that Roger Lathrop would open the
meeting with a speech similar to the one I'd
prepared for the recent news conference at the
Petroleum Club. Charlie Delman would then outline production plans for the future—which he'd
already worked out with Roger—and I'd follow up
with the new advertising campaign, ending with a
little motivational talk I'd used with other clients.

It was also decided that one of the regional
managers would be promoted to general sales
manager, and that the selection would be announced at the evening banquet following the
meeting.

Roger's comment summed it all up. "You can see
the kind of man Bart was when you realize that
now we need two top men to replace him: Charlie
Delman as head of production, plus someone else
to handle overall sales. As long as Bart was alive
we didn't have either, because he always did both
jobs."

As all this was being thrashed out—quite effi-
ciently, it seemed to me—Lisa kept refilling our

coffee cups. But with Sid Markowitz on my mind the whole time, the coffee did nothing to settle my nerves.

Finally, just as we were about to break up for the day, a phone call came in for me. Again, I took it in Dave Marshall's office. It was Laurie.

"I thought you were going to let me show you some of the sights," she pouted. "I haven't heard a word from you in three days!"

"I know, Laurie. But I've been busy."

"You can't stay busy all the time, Johnny. How about tonight?"

I thought for a minute. I'd made no other definite plans. "Why not? When do you want me to pick you up?"

"I don't know. What time will you get through at the plant?"

"I'm through now. Why?"

"Well, it's just after five. I could save you a trip and meet you at the Shamrock at, say, six o'clock. How about that?"

I thought again. "Sure, Laurie, that's fine. Call me from the lobby."

"I'll see you, Johnny," she said, and hung up.

We had been so engrossed in our plans for the sales meeting that I hadn't noticed the dark clouds gathering above the plant. Now, as I stepped outside, raindrops started to pelt the parking area. By the time I got to my car, there was almost a tropical storm, and all the way back to the Shamrock I found myself driving through what seemed like a solid wall of water. I felt as if I ought to file an instrument flight plan.

This time I pulled directly in front of the hotel

entrance. Why not? That's what doormen are for. I handed over a dollar and dashed into the lobby.

As I approached the door to my room, I heard what sounded like more heavy rain. Then, as I turned the key in the lock, I realized that the shower was running full blast. I remembered that I hadn't been in complete control of myself that morning—with good reason—but I couldn't imagine having left the shower on. Oh, well.

As I entered the room, the shower suddenly stopped. Laurie emerged from the bathroom, a towel around her tanned young body. It concealed her soft curves about as effectively as the tiny red bikini she'd worn—and not worn—that day in the Jeppsens' swimming pool.

"Laurie! In God's name. . . ."

"Johnny, don't be mad at me. I called you from Rice, and I just couldn't go out to dinner without cleaning up, could I?"

I shook my head helplessly. "But the door was locked. How did you get in?"

"The maid was very helpful." She grinned impishly. "I told you that money's to enjoy, didn't I?"

"Yes, but after all. . . ."

Laurie stepped directly in front of me. "Anyway, we don't have to go out to eat." She laced her arms around my neck and wriggled slightly, letting the towel slip onto the carpet. "Why don't we just order dinner in the room?"

Oh, hell. It was raining outside.

22

THINGS SEEMED QUITE NORMAL when I awoke the next morning. The operator called me at the appointed time; I was in bed and not in a pile of bushes alongside the hotel driveway; and there was no jackhammer pounding at the side of my skull. In fact, I felt great.

Then I heard the shower running once more, and I remembered. Laurie emerged a moment later, drying herself casually. When she saw that I was awake, she balled the towel up in one hand and held it above her head. Water droplets glistened on her skin.

She threw the towel at me playfully and said, "Your turn!"

I made a mock grimace. "Aren't there any fresh towels left?"

"Sorry about that. I used the other one last evening, remember?"

I grinned. "Okay. See you in a minute." I showered and shaved and then came back into the room.

Laurie was sitting in bed, a sheet up to her waist.

"That dinner last night was great," she said. "Let's order breakfast in the room, too."

"Okay with me." I reached the phone. "What do you want?"

"Bacon and eggs—whatever."

I placed the order and hung up.

"How long will it take them to bring it?" Laurie asked.

"About a half hour. Why?"

She kicked the sheet off the bed entirely and held out her arms. "That should give us time." She winked. "Otherwise I'll have to spend the entire day thinking blue."

Forty minutes later, as we started breakfast, I switched on the TV. The morning news was just beginning. As I'd expected, Sid Markowitz's murder was one of the lead items.

"Turn it off, Johnny," Laurie pleaded. "I don't want to hear about any more killings."

I started to bark at her, then realized that she didn't know my personal interest in the case. "Sorry, honey, I've got to hear this."

"But why? It's just another. . . ."

"I'll tell you in a minute, Laurie. Now *please*." She got the message and became quiet.

The TV screen showed what appeared to be a man's den. There was a small desk in the foreground, bookshelves in back, plaques of all shapes and sizes on the far wall, and an announcer with microphone off to the side.

"I'm speaking to you from Sid Markowitz's apartment on Chicago's near north side," he said. "This is where the well-known and widely beloved columnist and TV personality lived alone—and died alone yesterday morning, shot through the heart with a single bullet. The police say they have no clues in the case, except that it may involve the crime syndicate—how, we don't as yet know—and that Markowitz may have been on a long-distance telephone call at the time he was shot. To all the other questions that the world is asking, Chicago police are saying, 'No comment.' ''

I started to switch off the set, then hesitated as I heard the announcer continue talking.

"But there is one other strange aspect of the case," he went on. The camera zoomed in close on the announcer's strained face. "The coroner's office has released the fact that when Sid Markowitz's body was found, something was missing. *His tongue had been cut out.* And now, back to our studio. . . .''

This time I did switch it off. As I reached for my coffee cup, I had trouble holding it without spilling.

"God, Johnny," Laurie said. "What was *that* all about?"

"I'm not sure, Laurie. But it just may, in some way, have something to do with your dad's death."

Her eyes widened. "But how? I've never heard of Sid Markowitz. For God's sake, Johnny, tell me what this is all about?"

"Okay, Laurie. I guess I owe you that. Have you ever heard of a man named Marty Angel?"

"No. Who's he?"

"He's the rackateer Sid Markowitz was going after—the man who killed him, I'm sure."

"But that still doesn't explain what it's got to do with daddy—or you, either, for that matter."

"Laurie, *I* was the one Sid Markowitz was talking to when he got shot."

"Oh, my God!"

"And the reason he was shot was because he'd been given evidence that would convict Marty Angel."

"But I still don't see . . . ."

I reached across the breakfast table and held her hand. "Laurie, this is where it begins to hit close to home. Marty Angel is in Houston now. He's taken over most of the porno industry here. And— I guess you don't know this, but here it is—your brother owes him a big sum of money."

"Randy? How in the world would Randy ever get mixed up with something like that? He's never been mixed up with anything!"

"I'm afraid he has, Laurie—and he is." And then I told her the whole story about the Wahoo Lounge. As I'd expected, and hoped, it was all news to her. She'd known nothing about it whatsoever.

Laurie remained silent throughout my explanation of Randy's involvement with Marty Angel. She just sat there, shaking her head, totally bewildered.

Then she said, "I don't understand it, Johnny. I just don't. But it still doesn't mean that Randy killed my father!"

"No, it doesn't, Laurie. But it does say that he had a pretty good motive."

Just then the phone rang. I picked up the receiver. "Hello, Johnny McCoy."

"Mr. McCoy, this is Lieutenant Turlock of the Chicago Police Department. I'm calling you about Sid Markowitz's murder." His tone was polite, but direct.

"Yes, Lieutenant. That was a hell of a thing. Sid was a friend of mine."

"I know. His office said he was on the phone to you when he was shot."

"That's right. He was."

"What were you talking about?"

Again, I figured the time for confidentiality was long passed, so I told him about the evidence Sid had received regarding Marty Angel.

"Damn!" he said. "We sure didn't find any such evidence in the apartment. The killer must have taken it with him. Shit! Now we have to start all over again. Well, it isn't your problem."

"It is my problem, Lieutenant. I'm deeply involved in it, too." I went on to tell him about Randy Jeppsen's Wahoo Lounge, my encounter there with Marty Angel, and finally, the assault by Boris and company outside the Shamrock Hotel.

"I hope you don't pursue it any further, Mr. McCoy. From where I sit, it looks like it could be unhealthy for you."

He sounded genuinely concerned over my welfare. But my response remained as it had been ever since Bart Jeppsen's murder. "Sorry, Lieutenant. I'm in it too far now to back out."

"Okay. If that's the way it's got to be. But watch your step, will you?"

"I will, Lieutenant. Especially after last night. You can bet on that."

"All right. Take it easy. Oh, one other thing. Did Markowitz tell you who had given him all this evidence?"

"Not really. He was going to, but the shot rang out just at that moment."

"Then it could have been anybody. Damn!

Well, let me know if you find out anything else, will you?''

"Sure thing, Lieutenant. Sorry I can't be of more help." I broke the connection.

When I hung up, I noticed that the red message light was blinking. I picked up the receiver again and dialed the operator.

"There's a package here for you, Mr. McCoy," she said. "From Chicago. It just came in special delivery."

"Send it up, please. Right away."

A couple of moments later, a bellboy arrived with a small oblong package. He thanked me for the tip and left.

The parcel was several inches long, about the size of the Cross pen-and-pencil set that Marsha had given me last year for Christmas.

"What could that be?" Laurie asked.

"I don't know. Let's find out."

I slit open the wrapping paper with my door key and removed the cardboard box inside. I lifted the cover. Laurie almost fainted. So did I.

It was Sid Markowitz's tongue.

23

IT WAS SEVERAL MINUTES before Laurie and I even
began to regain our composure. If there had been
any doubt whatsoever about the meaning of
Boris's attack on me two nights earlier, the sig-
nificance of this was crystal clear. Marty Angel
was threatening me, not just with a lead-pipe
beating, but with death. About that, there was
absolutely no question.

I knew it would be a waste of time to report the
incident to Mendez, but Lieutenant Turlock had
sounded like a decent sort, so I decided to call him
back. It couldn't really serve any purpose to tell
him about it, but it certainly wouldn't hurt.

I'd neglected to ask him for his telephone number—and he'd forgotten to give it to me—but the
number was readily available through Chicago information. I dialed person-to-person, and after
just a moment he came on the line.

"Hello, Lieutenant," I said, "this is Johnny Mc-
Coy."

"Oh, yes," he came back. "I was just about to
call you."

"You *what*?"

"I said I was just about to call you."

"You just *did* call me!"

Now it was his turn to sound confused. "What are you talking about?"

Maybe I'm slow, but I still didn't get it. "Is this Lieutenant Turlock, in charge of the Sid Markowitz case?"

"That's right. And are you the Johnny McCoy who had lunch with Markowitz here in Chicago the day before yesterday?"

Then the light dawned. This *was* Lieutenant Turlock of the Chicago Police Department. The man I'd spoken with earlier *wasn't*. I hadn't been smart enough to verify his identity. Instead, I'd been dumb enough to spill my guts to him, even to the extent of telling him I intended to pursue my investigation. If Marty Angel had wondered whether I'd been scared off by the lead pipe, now he knew. And if I'd had any questions about *his* intentions, now *I* knew. Like Sid Markowitz, I was clearly marked for murder.

When I told Turlock what had happened—all of it—his immediate comment echoed my own thoughts. "I hope you realize you're not playing games, Mr. McCoy. There's no way we can keep you out of it—but neither can we guarantee to keep you alive."

"I'm aware of that, Lieutenant. But under the circumstances, I'll just have to take my chances. Do you want me to send this box to you, the one with the tongue?" I had difficulty even saying the word.

"No, it won't do us any good here. Just remember what it means."

The rest of our conversation went pretty much the same as the previous one with the other Lieutenant Turlock. Then we hung up.

Laurie was still shaking. She was curled up in an armchair by the window, sobbing softly, her makeup streaked with tears.

Finally, she spoke up. "Johnny, the police in two cities have apparently told you to forget this whole thing. Obviously, so has Marty Angel. Now *I'm* asking you. Please leave it alone!"

"Sorry, Laurie, I just can't do it." I stood beside the chair and stroked her blond hair. "I know you mean it, and I appreciate why you're saying it, really, but I've got to find out who killed your dad. I'm not going to let Marty Angel—or anyone else— push me around. You can understand that, can't you?"

She nodded, her eyes still filled with tears. Then, with effort, she straightened her shoulders. "Okay, Superman. But please be careful."

I grinned. "That's better. And now I've got to get to work."

"Will you give me a minute to put my face back on?"

"Sure."

Five minutes later, we rode down together in the elevator. The doorman brought my Cutlass and Laurie's Mercedes 450-SL. I kissed her tenderly, and we waved goodbye.

Back at the office, there were still some last-minute details to settle for the sales meeting. I had told Lisa exactly how I wanted the meeting room set up, and she verified that this had been arranged with the Lakeway office and all would be in readiness, including the cocktail party that was planned for Friday evening. The meeting itself would last all day Saturday, and Sunday morning

would be left open for golf, tennis and boating. As
Lisa had explained to me, Lakeway had excellent
facilities for all such activities.

Steve Fernley, the account executive at Jeppsen's ad agency, was due in later with layouts for
the new advertising campaign. Meanwhile, I had
two other phone calls I wanted to make.

The first was to Grundy Aviation. Again, Martha
Grundy answered.

"Hello, Mrs. Grundy," I said. "This is Johnny
McCoy. Is Jack there?"

"No, he spent the night again with his girl in
Corpus Christi. He's due back any minute. Why?"

"Well, I just wanted to make sure he finished
that twenty-five-hour check. I'm flying up to
Lakeway for the weekend, and we'll be leaving
around eleven tomorrow."

"Oh, that's a pretty place. You'll like it. Yes, he
did it the other day. I believe he's already signed it
off in the logbook, but I'll check with him again as
soon as he comes in."

"Fine. I appreciate it."

Then I thought of something else. Like most
instrument-rated pilots accustomed to making
long trips, I use instrument charts. They provide
the specific information you need for that type of
flying—airways, distances in nautical miles, minimum altitudes, radio facilities, etc.—but they
don't show terrain features. When I fly into
smaller, out-of-the-way airports, I prefer to carry
sectional charts as well, which are multicolored
topographical maps. They have less instrument information, but they do show cities, roads, lakes,
rivers, racetracks and all other prominent land-

marks—anything you can see and identify from the air. Unfamiliar as I was with the country around Lakeway, I decided they'd be helpful to have along.

So I asked Mrs. Grundy, "Do you have sectional charts that would cover the trip?"

"Certainly. We don't stock them for the whole country, but we always keep some on hand for this area. You'll want Houston and San Antonio. Lakeway is near Austin, but it's right on the edge of the San Antonio sectional."

"Good. I'll pick them up tomorrow before we leave. Thanks, Mrs. Grundy."

"Thank you, Mr. McCoy. We'll see you tomorrow."

My next call was to Howard Ketchum at the *Houston Post*. I caught him just as he was leaving for lunch.

"Hi, Howard. Johnny McCoy. Did you hear about Sid Markowitz?"

"Sure did, Johnny. Why?"

"Because he was after Marty Angel, too. That's why he was killed."

"Christ! Really? I hadn't heard that part of it."

"I doubted that you would have. It hasn't been made public."

"Then how did you hear about it?"

Once more, I related my visit to Chicago, my discussion with Sid Markowitz, the brief encounter with Marty Angel, the lead-pipe incident, the bogus telephone call from "Lieutenant Turlock," and all the rest, ending with my receipt of the tongue that morning.

"Jesus Christ, Johnny! That just about makes

you a bull's-eye, doesn't it? Are you still going to pursue it after all that?''

"Damn right. Now I'm starting to get mad.''

"Well, if it means anything to you, I'm not quitting, either. The cops don't seem to be doing anything about it. Somebody's got to.''

I breathed a sigh of relief. "That's what I hoped you'd say, Howard. Fact is, I'm going back to the Wahoo Lounge tonight. Want to go with me?''

"Sure, let's. Maybe we'll learn something else.''

"Great! What time do you want me to meet you there?''

He hesitated a moment. Then he said, "Well, to tell you the truth, I'd rather we went together. Tell you what. . . I live in Sharpstown, which is not too far from the Wahoo. How about picking me up around nine? We can go from there.''

"That's fine, Howard. Good idea.''

He gave me directions and we hung up.

Howard's suggestion was a good one. As things turned out, it wasn't good enough.

24

THE APPOINTMENT WITH Steve Fernley from the ad agency had been set for 1:30, so Roger and Charlie and I grabbed a quick lunch at a local drive-in. But, as so often happens with rush advertising jobs, the work wasn't finished exactly on time.

The phone rang at 1:45. "Hi, Johnny," Steve said. "Sorry I'm late. The artist is just finishing the last layout."

"We need 'em for the meeting, Steve. We're leaving tomorrow morning."

"I know. But you only gave us the assignment a few days ago."

"I realize that, Steve. And I appreciate your getting on it right away. But we still need 'em today. You knew that. Anyway, when can you get here with them?"

"It'll be late this afternoon. I promise. But don't hold me to a time. I'll be there as quick as I can."

I sighed. "Okay, I'll be waiting for you. Now, don't let me down!"

"I won't. See you later." He hung up.

Everything else was set, so I had nothing to do but twiddle my thumbs until he arrived.

At 4:30 the phone rang again. I grabbed the re-

ceiver, expecting to hear another apology from
Steve Fernley.

It was Laurie. "Hi, Johnny. How about dinner in
your room again tonight?"

"Can't do it, honey. I'm sorry."

The pout came into her voice again. "Didn't you
enjoy it last night?"

"Honest, Laurie, it was terrific. But I'm still
waiting for some ad layouts for the meeting. God
knows what time they'll get here. I may be stuck
for hours."

"All right. But let me know when you're ready
for an encore."

I grinned. "I'm ready now. But the ad layouts
aren't."

"Okay. Take care."

Steve finally arrived at 5:15. The layouts were
excellent. I put the portfolio under my arm,
stuffed my other papers into a briefcase and got
ready to leave.

Roger and Charlie had already said good-night—
they would be driving up to Lakeway in the morning—but Lisa was still at her desk.

"Hi," she said. "Remember me? I haven't seen
you for a while—except around here, I mean."

"I know, Lisa. It *has* been a while."

"Well, how about dinner tonight? If you're tired
of Pierre's there are other places."

I looked at my watch. It was almost six, so I had
three hours before meeting Howard Ketchum.
And I did have to eat. "Sure. Let's go someplace
else. Anywhere you say."

"Remember the first night you hit town, we had
a drink at Trader Vic's?"

"I sure do." It seemed like a long time ago.

"Have you eaten there yet?"

"No."

"Do you like curry?"

"Love it!"

"Then here's what we'll do. I'll follow you over there, so you won't have to drive me home. I'll meet you in the lobby. How does that sound?"

"It sounds perfect, Lisa. I'll see you there in a few minutes."

Lisa's Grand Prix was right behind me as I drove up the curved driveway leading to the Shamrock. I paid the doorman and asked him to park both cars. Once again, we walked into the Hawaiian atmosphere of Trader Vic's, stepped up into the cocktail lounge and ordered drinks from the same Oriental girl who had served us that first evening.

"It *does* seem like a long time, Lisa," I said. "I'm beginning to feel as if I belong here in Houston."

She smiled. "Everybody belongs here in Houston, Johnny!" She reached over and took my hand. "Especially people like you."

"You've never told me much about yourself. Is this your hometown?"

"It is now. But it wasn't originally. I'm really a small-town girl from Arkansas."

I laughed. "You don't seem very small-town to me."

"If that's a compliment, thanks. But that's the way Houston is—like New York, I guess, only more so. Practically everybody comes from someplace else."

"And you like it here, I take it."

"Darn right. If you can't make out in Houston—

and I don't mean just money—you can't make out anywhere. Anyway, this is the fastest growing city in the country. There's got to be a reason.''

"From what I can see, the biggest reason is men like Bart Jeppsen.''

Her face clouded for a moment. "Let's not talk about Bart tonight, Johnny. I'm here with *you*.''

I squeezed her hand. "That's nice, Lisa. And I'm here with you. But you still want to talk about the murder, don't you?''

"By all means. And I've got something to show you that may help. But let's do that over dinner.''

"Fine with me.''

We finished our drinks and stepped down into the dining room. The maître d' led us to a table by a window overlooking a lava-rock waterfall. Again, the whole place reminded me of a scene from "Hawaii Five-O.''

As the waitress brought menus, Lisa said, "Now, let me tell you about Trader Vic's curry. The su-su is mild. If you like the hot stuff, the way I do, you'll order the Calcutta.''

"That's for me.'' I nodded to the waitress. "We'll both have the Calcutta Chicken Curry.''

A little while later, the waitress brought out dinner. Alongside the curried chicken was a huge mound of rice, and almost surrounding the plate there was a crescent-shaped dish with little compartments filled with chutney, raisins, shredded coconut and other condiments. We both dived in hungrily.

"Okay,'' I said after a few moments. "What's this great thing you have to show me?''

"Here!'' Lisa reached into her purse. With a

theatrical flourish, she brought out a sheet of bond paper. "While you were waiting for Steve Fernley this afternoon, I was busy! Besides, I hate to keep ruining good menus." She handed it to me across the table.

The sheet was a sort of chart, a little bit like the charts they use for tennis tournaments. At the left, she had listed all the suspects: Cynthia, Randy, Laurie, Roger, Charlie Delman and Marty Angel. In the center, opposite each name, she had noted every possible motive. And finally, at the right, again opposite each name, she had put down the most likely method involved. The entire page was neatly typed, with ruled lines separating the columns.

I grinned. "Ever the efficient secretary!"

"Well, don't you think this might help us organize our thinking?"

"I'm only kidding, Lisa. Yes, it *does* put everything in perspective."

Then throughout dinner, we kept discussing the various possibilities. There was still no conclusive answer.

Finally, over dessert, I said, "The only trouble is that we're still back where we started. The chart's great, but all it really does is show us more clearly how confused we are!"

Lisa sighed. "I guess you're right."

"I'm afraid so, Lisa. But I'm not through trying. Maybe if I keep looking at this thing, some solution will emerge. Can I hold on to it?"

"Of course. That's what I made it for." She reached across the table again. "And now," she said, "let's stop talking about Bart Jeppsen and his murder."

"That's the best idea I've heard yet."

A few moments later, she said, "You know, you're a pretty special kind of person, Johnny."

"So are you, Lisa."

I wasn't kidding. Laurie was cute, pert and fun to be with. And she was certainly sexy. But there was something unique about Lisa. In a way, she was like the volcanic rock outside the window—lava that seethes and boils only at certain special times.

"Johnny," she said suddenly. "Do you remember when I asked you up for a nightcap and made it plain it was *only* for a nightcap?"

"Yes."

"Can I come up to your room now—*not* for a nightcap?"

I looked at my watch. It was after eight, and I wasn't sure how long it would take me to get to Howard Ketchum's house in Sharpstown. Damn!

"Lisa, this is the hardest thing I've had to say in as long as I can remember. But I have to meet a guy in a little while. We're going to the Wahoo Lounge together. It's important. So the answer is no. Not tonight."

"Oh, hell! Then pay the goddam check and let's get out of here!"

I couldn't blame her. But outside in the cool evening breeze, as the doorman ran to get our cars, Lisa put her arms around me and pressed her lips hard against mine. Her tongue searched deep in my mouth.

"Just wait till I get you at Lakeway," she said.

25

Following Howard's directions, I got on the Southwest Freeway and rode it all the way out to Fondren. On the right, as he'd said, was an immense shopping center with major stores of all kinds, plus a round, white theater that looked like a junior Astrodome. Turning left under the freeway, I found myself in an area of modest but attractive homes of varying architectural designs.

Once again, I was struck by a strange paradox: while Houston is a highly futuristic city, with ultramodern skyscrapers popping up all over the landscape, the residential areas seem anxious to recapture the past. Driving into Sharpstown, my headlights revealed houses that were American Colonial, English Tudor, French and Spanish Mediterranean, but very few with a contemporary flair.

Howard Ketchum's place was typical of most. A white picket fence ran around a small, well-tended front yard, behind which was a miniature one-story version of the Jeppsen's southern plantation manor. I stepped between the two white pillars guarding the front door and rang the bell. Soft chimes ding-donged inside.

Howard opened the door almost immediately

and ushered me into the family room, where two skinny kids were watching an old Elvis Presley movie on an almost equally old TV. Behind a breakfast bar on the far side, a small brunette was putting away the last of the dinner dishes.

"Nancy," Howard called, "come say hi to Johnny McCoy."

Nancy Ketchum came around the breakfast bar and held out her hand. "Hello, Johnny," she said. "So you're the great detective Howard's been telling me about."

I grinned. "Not very great at this point, I'm afraid. And not much of a detective. Just doing my thing for Jeppsen Oil Tool. Anyway, I'm happy to meet you, Nancy. Your husband is a dedicated guy."

"Sometimes too dedicated. But I guess I knew that when I married a reporter." She smiled. "Anyway, you two, don't get into trouble tonight." I suspect Howard had told her where we were going, but hadn't given her any of the details.

"You ready, Howard?" I asked.

"Sure thing." He picked his jacket up from a chair, then turned to the two youngsters curled up on the sofa. "Hey, you guys, isn't it time for bed?"

"Aw, dad," they answered in unison. "The show's not over yet." They looked up at Nancy. "Please, mom, can't we watch the finish?"

She shrugged. "Okay, but only for another half hour." The two kids settled back to their TV-watching.

Howard stepped over the sofa, pecked each kid on the cheek and came back to kiss Nancy. "Don't worry about us, honey," he said. "We'll be back in an hour or two." She walked us to the door, shook my hand again and we left.

Entering the Wahoo Lounge, I had a sense of déjà vu. The place was again thronged with male customers of all ages and types, including another quartet of drunk conventioneers with name tags. The same unkempt bartender was serving watered-down drinks; many of the same G-stringed girls were plying their trade; and the same sounds of heavy breathing and "ooh-aahing" were coming from the sofa in the back. On the small wooden stage behind the bar, Moira Lemoyne, whom I'd met that night in Randy's apartment, was twirling her G-string to the same loud disco music.

Without asking permission, and without bothering to cash in our ten-dollar beer chits, Howard and I stepped immediately into the narow hallway behind the bar. The bartender started to head us off, but then, seeing our expressions, just shrugged and gestured with his uplifted middle finger.

Approaching the office, we could hear another loud argument going on between Randy and Marty Angel.

"Look, punk," Angel was saying. "Don't hand me any of that shit about not being able to come up with the fifty grand now. Your old man was loaded. You'd better come across, or else."

"Marty, all I need is another few days. You'll get it, I tell you."

"That's what you said before, goddamn it!"

"I know, Marty." Randy was whining now. "But all I need is a few more days!"

Just then, the argument was interrupted by the ringing of the telephone. We could hear Randy answering it. "Wahoo Lounge.... Yeah, he's here. Who's calling...? Okay, keep it a secret." Then we heard him saying, "It's for you, Marty. I don't know who the hell it is. He wouldn't say."

Next came Angel's voice. "Okay, this is Marty Angel. What is it...? Oh, it's you. When are you going to bring me that stuff I asked for...? Yeah, you've been doing just fine on that end of it, but this is something that can't wait.... Why can't you get it here sooner...? All right, that'll have to do. Now, for God's sake, don't let it out of your sight! Deliver it to me *in person*. You got that...? Okay, see you then." Finally there was the sound of the receiver being slammed down.

I looked at Howard questioningly. He merely shrugged his shoulders. Meanwhile, Marty Angel was again turning his attention to Randy.

"Now, goddamn it, when are you going to come up with those fifty Gs?"

"Like I said, Marty, all I need is a few more days."

"Okay, Randy, here it is, and get it straight. When me and my boys play cards, we play for money, not promises. I was a schmuck to let you get behind in the first place—except you let me in on some of your action here at the club. Fair enough. But that doesn't wipe out the rest of it. You're still fifty thou in the hole and the string's run out. So I'll give you till next Wednesday at midnight. If I don't have the cash in hand by then, you've had it. And that's it, buster."

Howard and I looked at each other knowingly. Now we knew a bit about the relationship between Randy Jeppsen and Marty Angel, and at least a few of the details surrounding the debt that was owed. But how and why—or even if—this all tied in with Bart's murder, we still didn't know.

Meanwhile, Randy was saying simply. "Thanks, Marty. You'll get it, I promise."

It sounded as if a truce had been established, so before the argument could flare up again, I knocked and immediately opened the door.

"What the hell!" Angel started to say. Then, seeing me, he said, "Oh, it's you, McCoy. I thought I told you to. . . ." Then he noticed Howard Ketchum behind me. "Who the hell is that?"

"This is Howard Ketchum," I said.

Angel smirked. "Well, well! So you're the hotshot I can thank for that little publicity I saw in the *Post* last Sunday."

"That's right, Mr. Angel," Howard said. "And you're going to see more of the same as long as you're around here."

"Well, now, is that what you call southern hospitality? And I thought Houston was supposed to be such a friendly city!"

"It *is* a friendly city, Mr. Angel—to the right people. Your kind we can do without."

Then Randy tried to assert himself. He wasn't wholly successful. "I'll have you know I run a legitimate business here. And Marty is my partner. So I don't see what right you two have to come barging in here and berating us."

"We didn't barge in, Randy, and we're not berating you," I put in. "We're just paying you a visit to find out more about who killed your father."

That seemed to hit a nerve. "Dammit, McCoy, I told you before: I had nothing to do with that, and I don't know who the hell did!"

"What bothers me, Randy," I said, "is that you don't seem to care."

"I *don't* care at this point, and I don't want to talk about it. Now, for Christ sake, leave me alone!"

Marty Angel put it more succinctly: "In other words, gentlemen, fuck off!" Once again, the words came out like bullets.

"Okay," I said. I knew it would be a waste of time to ask him about the telephone call we'd overheard. "But there's just one other thing." I reached in my pocket and brought out the small oblong package that had arrived from Chicago. I handed it to Marty Angel. "I believe this is yours. I have no use for it."

Angel opened the box containing Sid Markowitz's tongue. He looked at it without expression and replaced the cover. "All right, McCoy. I get the message. I'm only sorry you didn't get mine."

"I got it, Marty. I just didn't hear it." Howard and I turned on our heels and left.

As we were walking out the front door of the Wahoo Lounge, Howard said, "I don't guess that did us any good, Johnny, but somehow I feel better."

"So do I." We started the car.

As before, cars were jammed tight against the

entrance, and I'd parked the Cutlass at the far side
of the lot, near the street. Approaching it, even
from that distance, I noticed that another gold
sedan, a Buick Regal, was parked alongside. They
looked almost like twins.

The four conventioneers evidently had left just
before we did. They were nearing the two gold
cars, laughing and jostling against one another,
almost falling down, singing "On Moonlight Bay"
in off-key harmony.

Apparently, but understandably, they mistook
my car for theirs. The conventioneer in the lead
opened the left-hand door of the Cutlass and stood
there for a moment, motioning to his buddies. One
of them got in the back, behind the driver's seat,
while the other two walked around to the other
side and started to pile in there. All four were still
laughing and singing at the top of their lungs.

Realizing that it was an honest mistake, I called
out jovially, "Hey, fellas, wait a minute!" Just in
case, I reached in my pocket and verified that I
still had the keys. No problem.

The conventioneers hadn't heard me. Three
were still crawling over one another to get inside,
while the driver remained outside with his hand
on the door. I called out again, "Hey, fellas!" They
still didn't hear. Or if they did, they paid no attention.

Howard and I were about twenty feet away at
that moment. It's damned lucky we weren't closer.

Three of the four men finally got themselves arranged in the car. The door on the far side
slammed shut. And then, at last, the driver
stepped inside and sat down. That's what did it.

Instantly, a huge orange ball of fire lit up the sky. The sound waves from the blast almost ripped up the pavement. Then it was over. It all happened in a split second.

My car and its occupants were a bombed-out rubble of ashes.

26

IMMEDIATELY, THE PARKING LOT was filled with people of all sizes, shapes and sexes in varying stages of dress and undress, as the Wahoo Lounge and its neighboring porno establishments disgorged the hundreds of patrons and staff who had heard the blast. Everyone was talking and gesticulating simultaneously.

The whole scene was like a circus sideshow when the lions and tigers get loose. Even Randy came out, his eyes glazed, waving and screaming meaninglessly. The only person not among the crowd was Marty Angel. I was not surprised.

Howard and I had seen enough. We dashed to the Sav-Mor service station up the street—which fortunately was still open—and I dropped twenty cents into the pay phone. My fingers had trouble finding the holes, but I finally managed to dial Mendez's number at Homicide. I didn't know whom else to call.

I sweated through three rings before there was an answer: "Hello, Homicide, Baxter."

"This is Johnny McCoy. Is Lieutenant Mendez there?"

"No, he's off duty. Cole and Nesmith are covering. What can I do for you?"

As quickly as I could, I told Baxter what had happened.

"Where are you now?" he asked.

"In the Sav-Mor gas station office at the corner of Richmond and Gessner."

"Of course, I know where that is. I'll have Cole and Nesmith come right out. So you just stay there and wait for them."

"We have no way to get home," I pointed out. "Should I call a cab in the meantime?"

"No way. The boys'll see that you guys make it home safely. So just sit tight where you are—and, for God's sake don't go back to the Wahoo Lounge. Okay?"

"This time I'll listen, officer. You can bet on that. Thanks a lot."

A short while later, we heard the wail of a siren, and then a blue-and-white squad car, with red light flashing, screeched to a stop outside the service station. Detectives Cole and Nesmith ran inside, quickly introduced themselves and instructed us to wait another few minutes while they inspected the remains of the Cutlass and asked preliminary questions. Howard and I did as we were told.

They returned moments later, shaking their heads.

"Boy, you sure weren't kidding about that car," Cole said. He was a tall young black man with handsomely chiseled features. "The damn thing—and everything inside—was practically cremated."

Nesmith was shorter and stockier, with a fair complexion and wavy brown hair. "And, as we might have expected," he said, "no one at the Wahoo Lounge volunteered any information at all."

"Did you talk to Marty Angel?" I asked.

"Sure we did. All he said was, 'Isn't that too bad!' So I guess we've got to ask you two: what do you guys know about it? It sure as hell wasn't an accident."

"How about letting us answer that one over a cup of coffee?" I suggested.

"Nothing wrong with that," Cole said. "I noticed a hamburger joint next door."

"If you don't mind," Howard put in, "I'd just as soon get the hell out of this neighborhood—for tonight, anyway. There's a Denny's in the next block."

Cole and Nesmith looked at each other, shrugged their shoulders, then nodded agreement.

Cole waited until the waitress at Denny's brought our coffees. Then he said, "I guess I don't have to tell you guys how close you came to getting killed tonight. So let's talk about it. First of all, what were you doing at the Wahoo Lounge tonight?" He shifted his gaze back and forth between us. "Neither of you looks like one of their typical customers."

"Thanks," I said. "We were just trying to find out more about the place. Ketchum here is a reporter." After the bouncing around that Sergeant Mendez had been giving me, I was reluctant to share more information then necessary.

Howard caught my drift. "That's right," he said. "I work for the *Post*. I'm doing a series on Houston's porno industry."

"Okay," Cole said. "I accept that for now. How long were you there?"

"Not very long," I said. "Maybe ten or fifteen minutes. Why?"

"Who knew you were coming?" Cole pressed on.

Howard broke in again. "Hell! What's that got to do with it? All we know is that while we were there, somebody rigged our car to blow up."

"That's what we're getting at," Nesmith put in. "The car *wasn't* rigged in the usual way. It couldn't have been. There wasn't time."

"What was it, then—spontaneous combustion?"

"Look, fellas," Cole said. "You were the intended victims, not the criminals. We know that. We're on *your* side. But we need your cooperation."

"You see," Nesmith explained, "there are lots of ways to rig a car. Most of them involve wiring the ignition, and that takes time. There's a faster way to do it, but that takes more preparation. And from everything you've told us—including the fact that you still had the keys—it's probably the method that was used here."

"Can you tell us about it?" I asked.

Again, Cole and Nesmith looked at each other, then nodded.

"Sure," Nesmith went on. "It's a technique sometimes used by foreign terrorists. At least, that's what we get from the reports. The way it works is this. You take a cardboard box—say a shoebox—and fill it with explosives. Then you take a small bottle, like a test tube, and fill it with concentrated acid and cork it tightly. You put the test tube in the shoebox, stick a spike through the cover, and then you replace the cover so that the spike almost, but not quite, touches the test tube. Again, all that takes preparation.''

My mind was racing. The subject of Bart Jeppsen's murder hadn't come up in this whole conversation, but I immediately began to wonder whether Nesmith's dissertation might not offer a clue to *that* bombing as well. But I said nothing as Nesmith went on.

''Anyway, all you have to do then is lift out the seat of a car, place the loaded shoebox underneath and then gently, *very* gently, put back the seat. The moment someone sits down, the weight drives the spike into the test tube, the acid hits the explosive and—pow!'' He spread his hands, almost like a lecturer anticipating his audience's applause.

''And that,'' Cole said, ''is probably how your car got blown up tonight. But it still doesn't explain why. So I'll ask you again: who knew you were coming to the Wahoo Lounge—and, even more importantly—who had it in for you?'' He looked at Howard. ''And I *don't* think it was just a case of vengeance against the media. His eyes swung back to me as he concluded. ''After all, McCoy, the car was *yours*. As I said before, we're on your side. Please don't hold out on us.''

I could see he had a point. And neither of these two cops were giving me the kind of runaround I'd gotten from Lieutenant Mendez.

So, once again, I related the whole series of events. I was beginning to feel like a telephone answering machine—except that each time the recording got longer. "Anyway," I concluded, "somehow I have a hunch that Bart was killed by either Randy Jeppsen or Marty Angel—or maybe both."

"That could be," Nesmith observed. "But why don't you let the police handle it?"

"Because they *haven't* handled it," Howard said. "Look, we appreciate you fellas coming out, and we're damn glad to get a lift home. But if the Police Department did its job, guys like Marty Angel wouldn't be operating in Houston."

"Now, hold it right there!" Cole said sharply. "No, we don't shoot our mouths off in public the way you newspaper guys do, but that doesn't mean we're not doing our jobs!"

"Wait a minute," I said wearily. "Howard and I are both a little uptight right now. You can understand why. But that's not what we're suggesting at all. We're just trying to help. As a matter of fact, I've tried to cooperate with your friend Mendez all along. I haven't found him the easiest guy in the world to work with."

Nesmith grinned. "I'll give you that, McCoy. But in his own way, he usually gets the job done."

"Do you two know what he's been doing, the facts he's uncovered in the case?" I asked.

"Of course we do," Cole answered. "We see the daily reports."

"Okay, then," I said. "What say we call a truce right here and compare notes? It could be helpful to everybody."

Cole and Nesmith looked at each other and shrugged. Finally Cole said, "That sounds reasonable enough, as long as you both understand that

we can't be held responsible for your safety."
Then he looked hard at Howard. "And as for you,
Ketchum, let's make sure *you* understand this is
all off the record. If I see a word of it in print, I'll
have your ass."

That broke the tension. "Fair enough," Howard
said.

"Deal," I agreed. "Now. I've told you what I've
been doing. And I'll tell you anything else I know,
as soon as I know it. So suppose you clue us in on
what progess Mendez has been making."

The waitress refilled our coffee cups as Cole
began. "Well, of course, he's talked to everyone
connected with the case, and he's had more than
one conversation with the obvious suspects. You
already know who they are."

"Right," I said. "The way I figure it, it probably
narrows down to Cynthia, Randy, possibly even
Laurie, though I doubt it, Roger Lathrop, Charlie
Delman or Marty Angel. They're the people with
the strongest motives."

Cole was obviously main spokesman for the
team, but Nesmith interjected again at that point.
"You've forgotten one," he said.

"Oh? Who?"

"Lisa Wallace."

"Oh, come on, now! She was in love with Bart!"

"Maybe," Cole said. "But then again, maybe
not. Sure, we know she was sleeping with the
guy—just as Roger Lathrop was making out with
Cynthia—but you never know what goes on
behind a bedroom door. Could be that Bart was in
the process of ditching her for someone else. She
wasn't the first fox he'd had on the side, you

know. Anyway, if she'd found that out, she might have done him in. More people get killed for passion than for money, don't forget that.''

Cole didn't know that the reverse was true, that Lisa had decided to drop Bart. Of course, she could have twisted the story a bit, and I *had* told her that I was heading out to the Wahoo Lounge. But to think of Lisa as a killer...that was crazy.

"I'm sorry," I said weakly. "But I can't agree. I just don't believe Lisa would ever do that. No way."

Cole and Nesmith glanced at each other knowingly. "Maybe that's an advantage of having professionals investigate crimes," Nesmith put in softly. "We don't get emotionally involved."

I threw up my hands. "Okay, let's leave that alone. How about Marty Angel? We know he was behind that assault on me the other evening. We know he killed Sid Markowitz. And he sure as hell arranged to have my car bombed tonight. Why can't you arrest him for all that? Then, if he's involved with Bart's murder, too, he might confess."

"Did anyone *see* him do all those things?" Nesmith asked, again in his soft voice.

"No, but..."

"Then forget it," Cole said. "Sure, you can press charges if you want. But you won't get to first base. Even if we tried to lock him up, his lawyer would have him out in an hour." He put down his empty coffee cup. "And so, gentlemen," he said, ending the conversation, "if you want a ride home, I suggest that now's the time."

Cole and Nesmith dropped Howard off at his

house in Sharpstown and then deposited me in front of the Shamrock. They'd shown me more cooperation than I'd gotten from any other member of the Houston Police Department, and it was nice to know that Lieutenant Mendez wasn't necessarily typical of the rest of the force.

The red message light on my telephone was blinking again. "Mrs. Cynthia Jeppsen called you at 9:20," the operator said. "It says here she wants you to call her back whenever you get in. The 'whenever you get in' is underlined."

It was well past midnight, but the message seemed clear. Cynthia answered on the first ring. Her "Hello" held no trace of sleepiness whatever.

"I'm sorry to bother you so late, Mrs. Jeppsen, but. . . ."

"That's all right, Mr. McCoy. Thanks for returning my call. I've got to talk to you as soon as I can."

I'd arranged to pick Lisa up at ten the next morning; we wanted to be at the airport by eleven and at Lakeway in time for lunch. So I hesitated a moment. Then I said, "What's it about, Mrs. Jeppsen?"

"Randy. I hear he's in trouble. Laurie told me all about it at dinner this evening. I'm worried sick! I never dreamed. . . . Anyway, that's why I need your help."

"Well, gee, Mrs. Jeppsen, I don't know. . . ."

"Look, Johnny—may I call you that? I know I wasn't very hospitable when you were here last week, and I'm still under a terrible strain. But Laurie's told me how you've been helping in the case—and what you've been going through, too—

and I want you to know how much I appreciate it.''

"That's all right, Mrs. Jeppsen. I'm just doing what I can.''

"That's exactly the point, Johnny. And right now you're probably the only person who can help. Could you come by the house tomorrow morning?''

"I'm not sure, Mrs. Jeppsen. I'm flying up to Lakeway tomorrow. We're holding a sales meeting there on Saturday.''

"Yes, I know about that. What time are you leaving?''

"Well, I'm supposed to—'' I caught myself in time "—I'm supposed to leave at ten.''

"Could you be here at eight? That would give us time to talk. Please, Johnny! It's terribly important to me!''

I gave up. "All right, Mrs. Jeppsen. I'll see you then.''

"Thank you, Johnny. God bless you.''

As I hung up, I wondered what I'd been conned into this time. In any case, I could see that all the Jeppsens were accustomed to getting their own way.

27

CYNTHIA JEPPSEN'S ATTITUDE was indeed vastly different than it had been the previous week. She greeted me at the door with almost as much warmth as my own mother had shown when I got home from Viet Nam.

"Oh, Johnny," she said, clasping my hand. "I'm so glad you could come. I know it was an imposition to ask you on such short notice, especially with the sales meeting coming up tomorrow."

"Not at all, Mrs. Jeppsen," I said. "I just don't know how I can help, though."

"I'm not sure, either. But I didn't know where else to turn. And from what I've heard, I have a feeling that you *can* help. Call it woman's intuition, if you like."

I shrugged. "I'll be glad to try." I didn't know what else to say.

"Have you had breakfast yet?"

"Yes, I ate at the Shamrock before coming out."

"Well, I'm having mine out by the pool. You can at least join me for another cup of coffee." It was a statement, not a question, the kind of statement she had probably made throughout her life. She called into the kitchen. "Sam, bring out an extra cup for Mr. McCoy, will you please?"

Without waiting for an answer, she led me out to the poolside patio where we'd first met. Her tan gabardine slacks rustled slightly as she walked. Looking at the pool, I could still visualize Laurie and her on-again-off-again bikini. But now the pool lay empty, the clear blue water unrippled by the soft morning breeze.

We sat at a round wrought-iron table near the bar, neither of us knowing quite how to begin. Cynthia Jeppsen brushed a hand across her sleek gray coiffure; she didn't find any hairs out of place. Then she said, "Johnny, what in the world am I to do? Randy has never done anything like this! We've always given him everything! How could he get mixed up in something like the— what's it called—the Wahoo Lounge?"

I didn't know how to answer, so I was glad that the arrival of breakfast gave me a moment to think. A slender Japanese man in a spotless white jacket deposited a tray in front of Cynthia and a cup in front of me. She thanked him in a matter-of-fact tone, her mind clearly on other things, and he padded silently back into the house.

I waited until she poured my coffee and took a sip of her own. Then I said, as gently as I could, "Randy has never done much of anything, has he, Mrs. Jeppsen?"

"No, I guess he really hasn't." She tried to smile, without much success. "But then, he hasn't had to. I'm sure you're aware, Johnny, that money has never been a problem with us, even lately, with inflation what it is." She started in on her shirred eggs, picking at them absently.

"Maybe that's been the problem, Mrs. Jeppsen.

Maybe if he'd had to get out and work for a living like everybody else, he would have."

She shook her head. "I suppose so. But that still doesn't explain it. Look at Bart. He could have retired the day he married me—I guess you've heard that, too—and certainly these last few years, he could have taken things a whole lot easier. He never did. He just kept driving himself, harder all the time."

"Yes, but that was Bart. We're talking about Randy."

"But Randy's our son!" Her voice began to rise, not in anger, but in desperation. "Bart would have taken him into the company at the drop of a hat!"

"You're still talking about Bart," I reminded her. "And about yourself. Randy's another human being, a whole other personality."

"But why, for God's sake? He's our own flesh and blood! If anyone ever had a chance to follow in his father's footsteps, it was Randy!"

"Now I think you've put your finger on it, Mrs. Jeppsen," I said softly.

She still didn't get it. "Put my finger on what, Johnny?"

"On the whole problem. Mrs. Jeppsen, have you ever heard of Billy Sunday?"

"No, I don't think so. Why?"

"Well, Billy Sunday was an evangelist back in the early part of the century—sort of a Billy Graham of his day. My grandfather used to tell me about him."

"What's he got to do with Bart and Randy?"

"Just this. My grandfather had a farm in Ohio. He always wanted my dad to go in *that* business

with *him*. Dad didn't care for it. Not to suggest
that gramp's farm was anything like Jeppsen Oil
Tool, or that my family ever had your kind of
money, but the situation was still pretty much the
same.''

''I still don't see what you're getting at! Please
don't talk in riddles, Johnny.''

''All right, here it is. One day gramp heard a sermon by Billy Sunday, and it changed his whole attitude. The main point of the sermon was: 'Don't
try to build your son in your own image. If the
good Lord had wanted it that way, He'd have
made you twins!' ''

''That's a clever line,'' she said. ''But I can't go
along with it, not in this case. Why *shouldn't* Bart
have wanted Randy to emulate his own success?
He was proud of his accomplishments, and he had
every right to be. No, he wasn't faithful to our
marriage—you already know that—but the whole
world looked up to my husband!''

''I know that, too, Mrs. Jeppsen. Your husband
was a truly great man. But it's possible that his
greatness was more than Randy could handle, that
the standard was just too high for him to meet.''

I felt I was making points, but Cynthia still
wasn't buying. ''And what's wrong with having
high standards?''

''Nothing,'' I said. ''But maybe we all need to set
our own. For instance, where did Randy go to college?''

''Rice. Bart wouldn't have sent him anywhere
else. That's where Laurie goes, too.''

''Exactly. And when Bart was there, he was
president of the student body, right? And he was

also was an all-American football player. Let's face it, Mrs. Jeppsen, your husband was a pretty tough act to follow.''

Finally, the light began to dawn. ''Yes, I guess he was. And I'll have to admit that Bart stepped on Randy pretty hard when he didn't even want to go out for the team.'' Her eyes widened. ''Maybe Bart *was* trying to build his son too much in his own image.''

I nodded. ''I never met Bart, Mrs. Jeppsen. You know that. And I've only seen Randy on a couple of occasions. But from everything I've heard, I'll bet that's exactly what happened. And when Randy didn't take to the idea of joining Jeppsen Oil Tool—where he knew he'd always stand under the shadow of his father—Bart probably lost all respect for him. So Randy lost respect for himself. Maybe this Wahoo Lounge thing was just another act of defiance against the family. Don't misunderstand me; I certainly don't approve of it. But maybe, under the circumstances, it wasn't really all that unreasonable. I'll bet Randy never really wanted all your money. He just wanted to be his own man.''

Cynthia Jeppsen's eyes were wet—not with grief, but with love and understanding. ''Oh, Johnny!'' she said. ''That's it! That's *got* to be it. How can I ever make it up to him?''

''I don't know how, Mrs. Jeppsen. But I think I know when.''

I said it because just at that moment, looking over Cynthia's shoulder, I could see a low-slung Porsche pull into the driveway. The young man who got out was Randy Jeppsen. He walked toward us hesitatingly.

Noticing my glance, Cynthia turned to look behind her. She got up, ran over to Randy and threw her arms around him lovingly. "Randy, darling!" she cried. "This is the first time you've been here since the funeral. I'm *so* glad to see you!"

"Hi, mom," he said. "It's good to see you, too. But I really wanted to speak to Johnny. I tracked Lisa down at her apartment, and she said he'd be here. Do you mind if we talk alone?"

Cynthia shrugged her shoulders in acquiescence; at that moment she was ready to agree to anything he wanted. But I wasn't. Randy was still a punk in my book, and very possibly a murderer. Nothing I'd said to Cynthia could change that.

"Now, hold it, Randy," I said. "If you have something to say to me, I'll be glad to listen. But not in secret. Whatever you've got on your mind, your mother has a right to hear it, too."

Both of them looked at me with new awareness. I suspected that Randy wasn't accustomed to hearing that kind of straight talk, even from his own parents. He hesitated just a moment, then nodded his head and sat down. Cynthia did the same.

"Okay, Randy," I said. "What can I do for you?"

"First, you can let me apologize," he said. "I've been doing a lot of thinking since last night."

He seemed ready, even anxious, to bare his soul, so Cynthia and I remained silent, waiting for him to go on.

"I guess you both know why I got into the porno

nightclub business in the first place." His eyes swung back and forth between us.

"Yes, dear, I think we do," Cynthia put in. "And, in a way, I guess your father and I were responsible. All I can say is. . . I'm sorry."

Randy waved a hand. "That's not the point, mom. What matters is that it took Johnny here to make me see how wrong I was." He turned toward me. "I've got to be honest with you, Johnny. At first I thought you were just sticking your nose in where it didn't belong. And even when Marty Angel had his goons rake you over in front of the Shamrock the other evening, it didn't bother me at all. But last evening, when your car got blown up and you were almost killed, I began to realize what was really going on. I've been up all night thinking about it." He straightened his shoulders. "So that's what I wanted to tell you. You were right, and I was wrong." He held out his hand. "Shake?"

I held out mine. "Shake, Randy. It takes a man to admit when he's been wrong."

Cynthia just sat there, her eyes glistening.

But I still wasn't entirely satisfied. "Just one more thing." I said. "It takes an even bigger man to do something about it. So the question is: what are you going to do with your life from now on?"

"That's something I haven't decided yet. But I intend to. I only know it will be something worthwhile."

"That's what I wanted to hear, Randy." I got up from the table. "And now, if you folks will excuse me, I've got to leave for that sales meeting."

Randy shook my hand again, and Cynthia kissed me on the cheek.

But as I headed my newly rented Cutlass toward Montrose Avenue and Lisa's apartment, I was still confused. Yes, apparently I'd been helpful to both Randy and Cynthia.

What I didn't know was: had I helped a murderer?

28

"WHERE THE HELL have you been?" Lisa demanded. "You're late!" She was standing in the doorway, hands on her trim hips, wearing a beige skirt and tailored blouse. A pale green scarf was wrapped around her dark hair.

"Come on, Lisa," I said. "You know where I've been—over at the Jeppsens'—and it's only a quarter past ten, anyway. We'll be at Lakeway in plenty of time." I kissed her on the lips, softly at first, then harder.

"Mmm," she said. "That's what I've been waiting for. Well, almost."

"Me, too. Let's get going." I picked up her slim overnight bag, and we headed down to the car.

"What this?" she said as I opened the trunk to put her bag in with mine. "A new car? What happened to the other one?"

I realized that the bombing probably hadn't made the early editions of the *Post*, and apparently Randy hadn't related the news to her, so I quickly reviewed the events of the previous night.

Lisa's dark green eyes widened. "My God, Johnny! You could have been killed!"

"That was the general idea." I grimaced. "And four other guys were killed in my place."

She shuddered. "I'm sorry about that part of it, too, Johnny. I really am. But you're the one I'm worried about."

As we headed out toward Hobby Airport, she again raised the question: "Why don't you give up, Johnny? It's just too dangerous. You've helped get Jeppsen Oil Tool back on track—that was the main objective. Why not quit while you're ahead? Maybe we'll never know who killed Bart."

My mind instinctively flashed back to Detective Cole's comment the night before—the fact that the police had listed Lisa, herself, as a possible suspect. Was that why she kept asking me to end my investigation of the affair? No, of course not! Impossible! Besides, it was Lisa who had urged me to take it on in the first place. She couldn't have done it!

"What are you thinking about?" she asked.

"Oh, nothing."

"Well, you don't know any more about it than you did at the start, do you? All you've done is almost get yourself killed... isn't that right?"

"That's right, Lisa," I said glumly.

"Well, then, what good is it to keep pushing your luck? Maybe one of these days it'll run out."

I glanced at her—so trim, so lovely—and shook off the mood. "Let's talk about something else."

She smiled. "Okay, let's. Tell me about dear Randy. What's the latest installment in that soap opera?"

I grinned. "You know, Lisa, there just may be some hope for that guy. I think he's about to get out of the nightclub business. That bombing of my car really opened his eyes to what's going on."

"Opened *his* eyes! What about *yours*?"

"I thought we were going to talk about something else!"

She held up her hands. "Okay, okay! Forget I mentioned it."

The drive to Hobby continued in silence.

But then, as always, as we finally turned onto Telephone Road, the airport sights and sounds began to quicken my pulse.

Once again, Martha Grundy was the sole occupant of the Grundy Aviation office and lounge. "Hello, Mr. McCoy, Miss Wallace," she said. "It's nice to see you again."

"It's good to see you, too," I said. "Don't tell me—Jack's away, seeing his girl friend again."

She smiled. "That's right! But he's got your ship all ready for you." She handed me the ticket, then said hesitatingly, "Mr. McCoy, I hope you understand. With the twenty-five-hour check, plus the gas, this is beginning to run up a little. It's been over a week and. . . ."

"Of course, Mrs. Grundy." I handed her my credit card. "Ring it up now, by all means. And don't forget to add those two sectional charts. Do you have them handy?"

"Oh, I forgot to pull them out, Mr. McCoy. You'll find them in the second drawer, over there." She pointed to an ancient black file cabinet in the corner of the office.

I fingered through the second drawer. As Martha Grundy had told me, all of the sectional charts for the area were in stock, filed alphabetically: Brownsville, Dallas-Fort Worth, Houston, New Orleans, San Antonio, etc., with WAC charts for

Mexico in the back. I withdrew the two that I needed—Houston and San Antonio—and closed the drawer. Signing the credit-card charge slip, I was again reminded of a thought I'd had many times over the years: the only thing in flying that doesn't cost a fortune is a sectional chart. They're a bargain.

My next step, as always, was to call the nearest FAA Flight Service Station to check the weather. The sun was shining clearly overhead, with only a few cottony puffs of clouds here and there dotting the sky. The weather was plainly VFR, but it never hurts to make sure.

"We're going up to Lakeway," I told the controller. "How does it look?"

"Well, Austin is showing 2000 broken, with 12 miles visibility. You should be able to make it VFR okay."

"Thanks," I said. "I'll call you right back."

The man was right, of course. It was VFR weather—meaning that it wasn't necessary to file an instrument flight plan—but I still hesitated. The sectional chart showed the altitude of Lakeway's airport to be 905 feet, so that 2000-foot layer of clouds at Austin would be little more than 1000 feet above Lakeway. And with higher hills all around, some of those clouds could have rocks in them. I decided to play by the rules.

I called the Flight Service Station and filed an instrument flight plan. I recited the usual litany of indentification, routing, altitude and all the rest, and then said, "I assume I can close my flight plan with Austin Approach Control, right?"

"Sure thing. No problem. Have a good trip."

As I hung up, Lisa said, "Well, are we ready to go?"

"Not quite," I said. "We've got to wait a half hour."

"For God's sake, why?"

"It takes that long to activate the flight plan, that's why."

"And what, pray tell, do we do during that half hour?"

"Well, for one thing, I check out the airplane."

"I thought Mrs. Grundy said that's already been done."

"It has. But I still want to check it myself."

She stared at me. "My God, you don't think there's any chance that Marty Angel could have rigged your airplane with a bomb, the way he did your car?"

I laughed. "No way. The security around airports is pretty tight. I just want to double-check the gas and oil."

She sighed with relief. "Oh, that's different. You had me worried there for a minute."

But she still followed me out to the ramp, where I loaded our suitcases into the baggage compartment and gave the Bonanza my standard preflight check. And thinking about what she'd said, I did give it more attention than usual. I looked around the door and up under the instrument panel. I even checked the inspection plates to make sure that the control cables hadn't been tampered with. Everything was in order.

"Well," I said, "the airplane's all ready to go." I looked at my watch. "But we still have a few minutes to wait. Let's do it inside where we can be comfortable."

Lisa dutifully followed me back to the Grundy Aviation lounge, where we sat down on a battered sofa. Like most people unfamiliar with aviation, she still couldn't understand the delay. I could. An airplane is not like an automobile—you don't just jump in it and go. That's the difference between piloting and driving.

As in all pilots' lounges, the coffee table in front of the sofa held an assortment of aviation magazines. One of them, a recent issue of *Flying*, immediately caught my eye. The cover carried a portrait of Charles Lindbergh, who was, and still is, the idol of private pilots everywhere. The story inside, titled "The Ocean-Hoppers," covered the flights of all the hardy souls who first flew the Atlantic and Pacific Oceans—exploits that still thrill all the rest of us. There was Lindbergh, of course, who made the first nonstop flight between New York and Paris; Clarence Chamberlin, who followed him across just a couple of weeks later; Maitland and Hegenberger, pioneers over the Pacific to Honolulu; Wiley Post, whose round-the-world flights beat all existing records; Amelia Earhart, whose disappearance over the Pacific still remains a mystery; and several others.

I was deeply engrossed in all this when Lisa said, "Hey, I thought you said a few minutes. Isn't it time to leave yet?"

I looked at my watch. "Right. Let's go." I put down the magazine, and said goodbye to Martha Grundy and ushered Lisa out to the Bonanza.

I fired up the engine, got our clearance and

taxied out for takeoff. Once again, there was that age-old thrill as the wheels lifted off the runway and tucked themselves neatly away.

"Lakeway, here we come!" I shouted in exultation.

"That's for me," Lisa agreed happily.

Now that we were finally on our way, we both relaxed, the tension was gone.

Of course, we couldn't know what lay ahead.

29

OUR ASSIGNED ALTITUDE was 8000 feet. The air was smooth, with only a slight headwind blowing from the west. White clouds, looking like blankets, drifted lazily below. Above, there was nothing but bright blue sky between us and God. Lisa and I held hands as the autopilot kept the Bonanza directly on course.

"Oh, Johnny," she said, all smiles now. "I'm sorry I bugged you this morning. But no more. This is going to be a great weekend, isn't it?"

"You bet," I said, and kissed her hard.

Nearing Austin, the radio controller instructed me to switch to Austin Approach Control. I tuned in, reported our position and confirmed that we were headed for Lakeway. We passed over the Austin Vortac and took up the new heading toward Lakeway.

"Bonanza 3682-Lima," the controller called. "Descend and maintain 4000 feet."

"Roger," I called back. "2682-Lima leaving eight for four."

"Understand you're going to close your flight plan with me. Is that affirmative?"

"Bonanza 3682-Lima. Roger, that's affirm. I'll let you know when I've got the strip in sight."

Moments later, the winding Colorado River opened up into Lake Travis. Between the clouds, I could see boats skimming over the waves. Then, slightly off to the left, the huge development that was Lakeway came into view. Lush waterfront homes dotted the shoreline for miles around and hundreds of others stretched far back into the hills. Then, at the center, the luxurious main lodge appeared. And beyond, just about a mile away, there was the paved airstrip.

Austin Approach still had us on radar. "Bonanza 3682-Lima," came the call. "Lakeway Airport is at eleven o'clock, eight miles ahead."

"3682-Lima," I answered. "Roger. We've got it. Would you close your flight plan, please?"

"Roger. Will do. Have a nice day."

"Same to you. Thanks a lot."

I switched to Lakeway Unicom, got the surface winds and told them we'd be landing in just a couple of minutes. I swung out over the lake, lowered the gear and turned back on final approach. Moments later, we touched down smoothly and rolled up to the parking area.

The Lakeway courtesy car was waiting for us. The uniformed driver loaded our bags into the station wagon, and we started off for the lodge.

After more than a week of Houston's pancake-flat landscape, the stark brown hills around Lakeway were a welcome relief. Curving roads, identified by blue and white pennant-shaped signs, wound through the property. The homes, unlike those in Houston, were mostly California contemporary in design. Natural stone, combined with redwood beams, gave them a delightful look of rustic elegance, and the rolling terrain provided vistas of the lake below.

Lisa radiated the excitement we both felt. "How would you like to own one of these?" she asked. "I mean, as a second home for weekends and vacations."

I grinned. "That wouldn't be hard to take, would it?"

"Well, you'll have to up your fees. Either that or start looking fifteen years ago."

"Prices a bit steep, huh?"

"Just a bit. When this area first opened up, you could have snagged the best lakefront lot in the whole place for around $10,000. You couldn't touch it now for ten times that amount."

Finally, the station wagon pulled up to the entrance of the low-slung main lodge. "I'll leave the bags in the car until we find out where you're staying," the driver said. "Then I'll take you down. Meanwhile, you just go in and register at the desk."

Lisa and I stepped into the lobby. I caught my breath: the place was gorgeous. To the left, a doorway opened into a lush warm cocktail lounge. To the right, I could see a large dining room lined at the side with an enormous smorgasbord. And all across the entire building, huge picture windows looked out over Lake Travis.

We registered at the desk, picked up our keys and went back outside where the driver was waiting. He drove us around the far end of the building and back down a road on the other side, past the swimming pool and a few tennis courts, to a series of cottages edging the lake. He deposited the bags in our rooms, thanked me for the tip and left.——

When I say "rooms," I am making a serious understatement. Lisa had arranged for them to be adjoining, of course, with an inside connecting door. But they weren't rooms, they were enormous suites. Each had a sitting area at one end, a wet bar with refrigerator in the middle and a huge round bed against the opposite wall. And each had its own private terrace overlooking the lake immediately below.

"Like it?" Lisa asked happily.

"Come here, woman," I answered hungrily. She melted into my arms.

"Just a minute," she said a short time later. "It's celebration time." She opened her suitcase and brought out a bottle of champagne and a corkscrew. "Here," she said, handing them to me. "You open it while I get some ice."

"Woman, you think of everything."

I popped the cork while Lisa busied herself with glasses and ice. She brought them over to me and I poured. The bubbles seemed to mirror our mood.

"Here's to the weekend," I said, lifting my glass and clinking it against hers.

"To *our* weekend, Johnny."

"How about lunch?" I asked a few moments later.

"What time is it?"

"A little after one. Why?"

"They don't stop serving until two," she said. "So there's something else we can do first."

"What?"

"You know what. Just wait for me a minute, will you?"

"I've waited over a week, Lisa."

She kissed me again and disappeared into the adjoining room.

In a moment she was back, wearing her green scarf and a smile.

"It's kind of silly to keep this thing on, isn't it?" she said.

She withdrew the scarf and softly, sweetly lowered her lithe body onto the bed.

30

WE MADE IT to the dining room just in time. As we arrived at the sumptuous buffet table, the last of the other late stragglers were picking up their desserts. We sneaked in quickly behind them, and then the rope went up, ending meal service until dinner.

But once we had our plates filled with a variety of salads, cold meats and hot roast beef and vegetables, we were able to eat and relax at leisure. As before, I was struck by the casual elegance of the entire place.

"This is a great spot, isn't it, Johnny?" Lisa enthused.

"Sure is," I agreed. At that moment, the still unsolved riddle of Bart Jeppsen's murder seemed light-years away.

We were halfway through lunch when Roger Lathrop's brisk voice echoed through the dining room. "Hello, Johnny! Hi, Lisa!" He and Charlie Delman came over, pulled a couple of chairs from a vacant table nearby and sat down with us by the huge picture window overlooking Lake Travis.

"Glad to have you join us," I said. "But I'm afraid you're a little late for lunch."

"No problem," Charlie said. "We ate along the

way." He signaled to the waitress. "But I could do with another slug of coffee."

As the smartly uniformed girl poured two more cups, Roger asked, "Have you checked out the meeting room yet?"

"No," I said. "We were going to do that now."

"There's plenty of time," Roger said. "Why don't you two wait here for a few minutes. Give Charlie and me a chance to unload our bags, and we'll be right back. Then we'll look it over together."

"Fine," I agreed.

They drained their coffees and walked back out to their car.

Roger and Charlie returned a few moments later, both dressed in casual sport shirts, slacks and loafers. As they came through the dining room together—Charlie long and lean, Roger short and pink-cheeked—they reminded me of a Mutt and Jeff cartoon.

Lisa had reserved the meeting room for that day also, so we knew it would be available for our inspection and preparation. All was as she'd arranged. So, as the Lakeway courtesy car deposited other members of the group in front of the lodge, we spent the remainder of the afternoon supervising the setup of tables, chairs, lectern, blackboard, easel, flip-chart and all the other vital paraphernalia for a successful meeting. By five o'clock, all was in readiness.

"I'm beginning to feel a little grubby," I told Lisa. "I think I could do with a shower."

She looked at me solemnly. "So could I, Johnny."

We walked down to our rooms, stripped off our clothes and luxuriated together under the warm needlepoint spray from the showerhead. As I'd long suspected—and had confirmed only a few hours earlier—beneath Lisa's veneer of cool reserve lay an almost animallike lust. There was no sham, no pretense, just the sheer, unadulterated joy of giving and receiving ecstatic pleasure.

When we arrived back at the lodge, an informal cocktail party was in progress in the bar. Roger introduced me to the regional managers and district managers from the various offices around the U.S. and Canada—New Orleans, Lafayette, Midland/Odessa, Oklahoma City, Denver, Akron/Canton and Edmonton—all of them active centers for oil drilling activity. Of course, I'd already met Dave Marshall, who had flown in from Europe the day before. Once again, it became apparent that the petroleum industry is populated by men who work hard and play hard, and do both exceedingly well.

During the third round of drinks, Roger sidled up to me, glass in hand. "What do you think of our little group, Johnny?" he asked with obvious pride.

"Looks like a great bunch," I said.

"Any ideas who'd make the best general sales manager?"

"Too early to tell. Let's see how they all perform at the meeting tomorrow."

Roger nodded. "Check."

Finally, just after eight o'clock, the group gravitated into the dining room, where two long tables had been reserved for the Jeppsen party. The dinner consisted of salad, thick New York steak and baked potato, with apple pie à la mode for dessert.

It was almost ten before Lisa and I could make our exit. We had a short nightcap from the champagne bottle, then tumbled into bed.

"Ready for another nightcap?" Lisa asked.

"I don't know, honey. I think I've had enough to drink for one evening."

"That isn't what I meant," she said.

A half hour later, we were both sound asleep.

THE MEETING STARTED promptly at eight o'clock the next morning. Most of the men, I learned later, had played poker well past midnight—some of them until three in the morning—but all were ready and alert when Roger opened the proceedings.

"You all know why we're here," he said. "Not to dwell on the past, but to discuss our future together, a future that's as bright as we make it." And the speech continued in that vein, much like the one I'd written for the news conference at the Petroleum Club over a week earlier.

Then, about 8:20, Roger brought out a series of charts, which he placed on the easel to his right. "Please understand," he said, "that these charts were *not* prepared for this meeting. They show the projections that were drawn up before the tragic event of less than two weeks ago. But here's the point: these projections are still valid, and *they will be realized*. That's the way Bart would have wanted it . . . that's the way everyone here today wants it . . . and that's the way it's going to be!"

The men remained silent and solemn-faced, but it was obvious that Roger commanded their attention, and their approval.

For the next hour, Roger explained the sales and profit figures on the charts, adroitly fielding the various questions raised by the group. Again, he looked and sounded like a man in total control. Finally, he dropped the bombshell we'd discussed earlier. "There's just one more thing," he said. "As you all know, we at Jeppsen have never had a general sales manager, only because Bart himself always assumed that role. But now it's evident that we need one. And one of you will be selected for that job. Your records and the performance figures of your respective regions have all been reviewed. The final decision will be made later to-day, after the conclusion of the meeting. The announcement will be made at the banquet this evening." The group stirred visibly.

Then it was time for coffee. The men milled around, talking in animated voices, clearly pleased with what they'd heard and seen so far.

Next, it was Charlie Delman's turn to occupy center stage. After Roger's warm introduction, he rose and stood behind the lectern, awkwardly at first since he was a man of action more than words. But then, sensing the favorable response, he forgot his inhibitions and presented a concise, logical description of the new products being developed in the plant and their vast applications worldwide.

With all the questions that Charlie's discourse generated, his presentation lasted almost two hours. The most piercing comments came from a stocky man in the front now. His name tag read, "Dan Trimble." Several times I caught Lisa's eye, and she nodded approvingly. With Bart gone,

Charlie Delman's appointment to the corporate staff *was* superb strategy on Roger's part. And among the regional managers, Dan Trimble appeared to be the natural leader.

"If there are no more questions," Charlie concluded, "let me just say that I'm fully aware of the drilling difficulties that exist in various parts of the world. But in all areas, when you sell Jeppsen you're giving your customers the best, and we'll always continue to honor that pledge."

For the first time, hearty applause rang through the room. Then the meeting broke for lunch.

That afternoon, I presented the ad layouts that Steve Fernley's agency had prepared, explaining how this new program emphasized the same point brought out earlier—that Jeppsen was a leader customers could count on. Then I launched into my little motivational windup.

"Gentlemen," I said, "you're aware that I'm the new kid on the block. Many of you have been in the oil patch all your lives. I haven't. So you know ten times as much about the industry as I ever will. But let's talk for a few minutes about some basic things we can all do—in any business—to become just a little more effective in our jobs." And I went on to hit some age-old truths that everyone has heard before, but many people tend to forget.

"The point, it seems to me," I concluded, "is that maximum success for any company comes when everybody does his best. And from what I've noticed here today, that's what's going to make the future for Jeppsen Oil Tool. For each of us, the answer lies in what we see in the mirror."

Roger then had just a few final remarks, and the meeting broke up amid renewed applause. By all odds, it was clearly a bang-up success.

Since there were still two hours remaining before the evening cocktail party, some of the men ran off to get their tennis rackets, others their golf clubs, still others their fishing gear.

Lisa and I had a different idea.

Later, while the cocktail party was in progress, I had a chance to huddle briefly with Roger and Charlie.

"Have you decided on the new general sales manager?" I asked Roger.

"I think so," he answered. "But I'd like to hear your own recommendation first."

"So would I," Charlie agreed. "Who would you pick, Johnny?"

"Why don't we do this," I countered. I ripped a sheet of notepaper from my pocket calendar and tore it into three pieces. "Let's each write down our own choice," I suggested. "If we agree, there's no need to discuss it further. If not, we can talk about it more."

"Fair enough," Roger said.

"Good idea," Charlie chimed in.

The decision was unanimous: Dan Trimble, Regional Manager in Denver.

Two hours later, over dessert, Roger made the announcement. He got to his feet and clinked a knife against his water glass. "I've got something to tell you fellas," he said. "First, I want to thank you all for your participation in the meeting today. I think it was a big success, don't you?" There was enthusiastic applause. "In particular," he went on, "I want to thank Charlie Delman for his fine contribution." More applause. "And, certainly, we all owe a vote of appreciation to Johnny Mc-Coy, who planned the whole meeting." More applause. "And, especially, for her enormous help behind the scenes, my thanks to Lisa Wallace." Still more applause. "And finally, I need to tell you that we're going to be looking for a replacement in the Rocky Mountain Region." A few of the men looked startled. "For this is to announce the new general sales manager of Jeppsen Oil Tool is. . .Dan Trimble!"

From the enthusiasm that greeted Roger's announcement, we could all tell that our decision was a good one.

The festivities continued well into the evening. Again, I could see that Jeppsen Oil Tool was indeed embarking on a bright new phase of lasting prominence in the industry.

But that night, nestled in Lisa's arms, I was once more nagged by the memory of the staggering events that had brought all this about. And I couldn't help wondering what else would have to happen before we'd learn who had killed Bart Jeppsen.

The answer to *that* question, at least, was not long in coming.

31

Sunday dawned clean and clear. Drawing back the draperies that covered the picture window, I could see bright sunlight reflecting off Lake Travis. Far in the distance, the sails of small boats dotted the horizon, and weaving a path among them, a water-skier was skimming across the waves.

"How about some breakfast?" I asked Lisa. "I'll call room service, and we can eat on the terrace."

An hour later, we were downing the last of our scrambled eggs.

"What now?" I asked. "We've got all day before we have to leave."

"I thought you might enjoy seeing more of the lake," she said. "While you guys were stuck in the meeting yesterday, I ducked out and reserved an outboard for 9:30 this morning."

Lisa led me down the paved driveway in front of cottages and along the bluff overlooking the lake. In her trim white tennis shorts, she looked almost like a college sophomore.

"That water is still at least a hundred feet below us," I observed. "How do we get down there?"

"Just a minute," she said. "You'll see."

A moment later, we came to a redwood-decked platform surrounded on three sides by a rustic wooden shed. Two parallel iron rails, about three feet apart, stretched perpendicularly down the bluff to the water. The angle appeared to be about forty-five degrees. Lisa pressed a button on the wall of the shed, and a little red cable car, big enough to seat four people, left the water's edge and whined its way up the embankment. With an audible groan, it finally jerked to a stop alongside the platform.

I gasped in amazement. "Wow! What will they think of next!"

Lisa and I climbed aboard the cable car, she pressed another button, and the little car whined back down the rails. Just as it seemed about ready to slide into Lake Travis, it again jerked to a stop alongside another small platform at the bottom. This led to a large floating marina, with boats of all kinds and sizes tied up in rows of slips. Finally, at the far end, there was a brightly painted building that served as the marina office.

A blond young man in sweat shirt and blue denims greeted us in the office. The front of his sweat shirt was lettered, "Texas A & M."

"Hi," he said cordially. "Can I help you?"

"Yes," Lisa spoke up. "I believe you have a boat waiting for us. I'm Lisa Wallace and this is Johnny McCoy. I phoned yesterday."

He ran his fingers down a clipboard on the counter. "Sure thing," he said. "I've got an eighteen-foot MerCruiser for you. Will that be all right?"

Lisa looked at me questioningly.

"That'll be just fine," I said, signing the ticket.

The young lad from Texas A & M led us out to a

handsome white boat moored in a nearby slip and handed me the keys.

"That's a fine-looking craft," I said.

"It really is," the kid agreed. "The best we've got—for rent, I mean. You sure you know how to run it?"

"No problem," I assured him. "I was checked out in one just like it a few months ago." Knowing that boats like that cost real money, I could understand his concern.

"Okay," he said. "Have fun!" He untied the boat, coiled the painter around a stanchion on the forward deck, waved goodbye and trotted back to the office.

Lisa and I climbed aboard. I started the engine, let it idle for a moment and put it in reverse. The boat purred softly toward the open lake, I eased in the throttle and the engine swelled to a throaty roar. Seconds later, we were speeding westward along the shoreline, past the hundreds of luxurious vacation homes that spread out above us on the bluff.

Lisa had left her scarf in the room, and her long brown hair was now flying in the wind. "Hey, hey!" she yelled above the roar of the 140 horses propelling us through the blue waters of Lake Travis. "This is neat!"

I just looked at her and grinned.

We cut directly across the lake toward rows of other homes on the other side.

"What's that?" I shouted, pointing. "More of Lakeway?"

"No," she yelled back. "That's Point Venture. A whole other development."

I turned the MerCruiser westward again, along the far shore. After a while, the houses disappeared, and the stark Texas hills stretched out on all sides. The lake finally began to narrow into a long, curling finger.

I throttled back and let the boat slow down gradually. The engine again became a contented purr.

"This *does* look like a river," I commented.

"That's what it is—or would be if it weren't for the dam back at the other end. But now it's a lake. Just think what God could have done if He'd had Texas money!"

I laughed.

We were now cruising slowly, almost silently, into a deserted cove. The beach looked smooth and clear of rocks, but I decided not to take any chances. I shut off the engine and threw out the anchor.

"Gee, this is fun, Johnny," Lisa said gaily. "How about a swim?" Without waiting for me to answer, she stripped off her tennis shorts, shirt, bra and panties and dived overboard. I followed without hesitation.

For the next twenty minutes, we frolicked together in the water, totally oblivious to the world around us. Once again, I forgot entirely about murders, amputated tongues and blown-up cars and helicopters. They didn't exist. I was on another planet.

At last, we climbed aboard the boat and stretched out, side by side, to let the warm sun dry our bodies. Then we slipped back into our clothes, and I started up the engine and headed the MerCruiser back toward the Lakeway marina.

The blond kid from A & M was waiting for us. As he tied up the boat, he asked, "How was it?"

"Fantastic," I said. I gave him a very generous tip. It wasn't enough.

Lisa and I enjoyed another delicious buffet lunch. Then we packed and checked out.

As the driver was loading our bags into the courtesy car, Roger Lathrop and Charlie Delman were just coming off the tennis court. They were both sweating profusely, but grinning like schoolboys.

"Are you two heading back already?" Roger asked.

"Might as well," I answered. "This has been just great, but it's about that time."

"Well, Johnny," Roger said, "I want you to know how much I appreciate all the help you've been to us."

"Me, too," Charlie echoed.

"Glad to do it," I said. "I'll see you in the office tomorrow." Lisa and I waved goodbye and got in the car.

Driving to the airstrip, I began to notice that a few clouds had begun to gather overhead. I phoned Austin Flight Service Station from the Lakeway Airport office and was advised that Hobby was showing 1500 feet overcast, with light rain and seven miles visibility.

"Their forecast calls for the weather to go down somewhat," the controller said. "It looks like about 1000 and five later this afternoon. Are you instrument-rated?"

"That's affirmative," I answered. "Can I file a flight plan with you?"

"Sure. Go ahead. You can call Austin Radio to activate it after you get airborne."

Once again, I rattled off the necessary information. I told the man we'd wait the normal thirty minutes and then take off at 2:15. He gave me the clearance and I read it back as usual.

"That's fine," he said. "Have a good trip."

This time, now becoming accustomed to the procedure, Lisa didn't complain at all. After the weekend we'd just enjoyed, neither of us was complaining about anything. So, waiting for the clearance to be put through, we just sat there in the office, talking about everything in general and nothing in particular. Then it was time to go.

I gave the Bonanza a quick preflight check, loaded the bags, and we got aboard. Once more, we roared down the runway and into the air. I banked over the lodge, waggled the wings twice to say goodbye and winked at Lisa. Then, gaining altitude, I switched to Austin Radio and called them to activate our flight plan.

"Roger, Bonanza 3682-Lima," the voice came back. "Your flight plan is activated. Climb and maintain 7000."

"Roger, Austin," I said. "3682-Lima is leaving 1500 for seven."

Shortly after passing Austin, the clouds beneath us began to thicken, and about halfway to Houston, as predicted, the weather below became solidly overcast. Soon, higher buildups appeared directly ahead. The clouds were no longer white puffs of cotton. They were dark, angry and menacing, and off to the north, jagged streaks of lightning lit up the sky. A minute later we were in the stuff, flying blind, bumping along like a runaway wagon on a rocky prairie. A couple of times, we hit down drafts that almost made us bang our heads against the roof of the cockpit. Hard rain began to pelt the windshield.

I sneaked a glance at Lisa. She was saying nothing, obviously not wanting to interrupt my concentration. Even with the autopilot on, she could see that I was busy. But her lips were clenched tight, and her hands, gripping the sides of the seat, were white and sweaty. I wasn't too happy myself. I'd been through worse storms—plenty of times—but flying through severe weather is never fun.

Still, we seemed in no real danger. There was no threat of ice, the autopilot kept us on course, the instruments were all functioning normally, and I had no trouble maintaining radio contact with Houston.

About fifty-six miles out, passing Navasota, the controller said, "Bonanza 3682-Lima, switch to Houston Approach Control, 124.35."

"3682-Lima, Roger." I answered. "Houston Approach 124.35."

I switched frequencies as instructed and called out, "Houston Approach, this is Bonanza 82-Lima, at 7000."

"Roger, 3682-Lima," the voice came back again. "82-Lima, descend and maintain 2000. Switch to Houston Approach, 119.1." I rogered back and made the change.

"3682-Lima, leaving three for two. What's your weather at Hobby now?"

"It's down to eight hundred and three. Wind one-four-five at eighteen, gusting to twenty-five. Altimeter two-nine-nine-seven. You're cleared for

the ILS, runway one-three. Switch to tower crossing the outer marker, one-eighteen-point-seven.''

"Roger," I called, reading back the clearance.

We were still in the soup, of course, but the
bumps had smoothed out somewhat, and the rain
had softened. The ceiling and visibility were
perfectly acceptable for an instrument landing—
far above minimums—so my concerns began to dis-
appear. Even Lisa appeared to relax somewhat.

Then, just a couple of minutes later, it happened. It was something I was totally unprepared
for—couldn't have been prepared for. But it happened.

I'd been following instructions to the letter,
keeping the Bonanza precisely on the prescribed
course, descending exactly as called for. Intersect-
ing the localizer beam, I turned onto final approach and lowered the gear and flaps. Keeping
both needles centered for localizer and glide slope,
I began our final descent onto runway thirteen at
Hobby Airport.

When the ADF needle swung around, indicating
our crossing of the outer marker, exactly 5.2 miles
from the runway, I switched to the tower fre-
quency as instructed and called out, "Bonanza
3682-Lima, outer marker, inbound for runway
one-three."

Still unable to see even as far as the wingtips, we
continued our descent. The altimeter needle un-
wound as we neared the ground.

A moment later, a voice came back. "This is
Hobby Tower. Bonanza calling, say again."

"Bonanza 3682-Lima. Just passed outer marker,
inbound for runway one-three."

The voice came back more urgently. "Bonanza 3682-Lima, say your altitude."

"3682-Lima descending through 900."

This time the voice literally screamed at us. "3682-Lima we show you twelve miles northwest! Pull up! PULL UP!"

I reacted quickly. But almost not quickly enough.

By the time I applied power and pulled back on the stick, we were down to 850 feet. And by the time the *airplane* reacted, we were below 800.

Just at that moment we broke through the overcast. For the first time in over a half hour, we could see outside. Lisa let out a terrified scream. I didn't blame her. For there, directly in front of us, just a few hundred yards away, approaching at almost 200 miles an hour, was the Exxon Building! That's right. The Exxon Building! And I mean it was right *there*! We were still over the center of downtown Houston!

I flipped up the landing gear and banked hard to the right, applying every ounce of power possible. As we veered away, the left wing tip practically scraped the picture window of the Petroleum Club.

Just as we passed, I could actually see two men in business suits staring at us through the window. They dropped their Scotch and sodas.

I almost dropped something else. In my pants.

32

THERE IS AN OLD ADAGE among pilots: "avigate, navigate, communicate." What it means is that navigation, directing your course through the sky, necessarily takes precedence over radio communication with the ground—but the *first* thing you have to do is fly the airplane.

So the renewed screams from the tower were of minor concern. I simply ignored them. I was too busy getting the Bonanza under control. And instinctively realizing that my instruments must have gone out at the critical instant just before crashing into the top of the Exxon Building, I was not about to climb back into the soup as the controller had advised.

Instead, I simply maintained altitude just below the overcast and dodged my way around the remaining skyscrapers at the southern edge of Houston's downtown business district.

Just a few minutes later, Hobby Airport came into view. Then I called the tower and executed a normal landing. Lisa was still trembling like a windup teddy bear. My own palms were wet.

Taxiing in to the Grundy Aviation hangar, I got another radio call from the ground controller. His voice was now calm and his words were measured. "Bonanza 3682-Lima," he said, "please report to the tower—in person—as soon as possible."

"Sorry," I told him. "I'll send you a written report tomorrow." I could see that Lisa needed to get away from the airport right away. So did I. All I wanted at that moment was to get the hell out of there and into a stiff double Scotch.

We drove back to Lisa's apartment in almost total silence. Neither of us had to express the emotions we both felt.

As I parked in front of the Montrose Avenue apartment building and reached into the back seat for Lisa's bag, she pointed to mine and said, "Do you have another change of underwear in there?"

"Sure."

"Then bring it along," she said.

Once inside the apartment, we fell into each other's arms. We remained in a tight embrace for several minutes. Finally, without urging on my part, Lisa poured two stiff drinks. With difficulty, we brought our glasses to our lips.

Then, and only then, did she seem capable of almost coherent speech. "I know you did a fabulous job out there, Johnny." Her shoulders were still quivering, her hands still shaky. "But if that's what flying's all about, I don't want any more of it, thank you. I've had enough."

"It *isn't* like that, Lisa. Not normally. Something happened. I don't know what—not yet, anyway—but it was certainly something out of the ordinary."

"Out of the ordinary! My God, I hope so! Anyway, if it's okay with you, let's not talk about it."

"Fine," I said. "Let's talk about dinner. Where do you want to eat?"

"I don't think I'm very hungry, Johnny."

"Then let's just wait a while. Maybe we'll both feel better after a few minutes." After many thousands of hours in the air, I'd learned that fear, like pain, has a short memory.

A half hour later, as I'd expected, we began to relax. So I asked again, "Are you sure you don't want something to eat?"

For the first time in over two hours, Lisa managed to smile. "Why not?" she said. "Maybe Pierre's *Poulard Marseilles* would just hit the spot."

"That's my girl."

Once more, Pierre greeted us enthusiastically and led us back to the same table we'd occupied that first evening together. Again, it seemed like a long time ago.

Threading our way through the round tables, we spied a couple near the far corner who were holding hands and grinning at each other like teenagers at a senior prom. With their eyes locked together, they were totally oblivious to the sights and sounds around them. It was Laurie Jeppsen and Steve Fernley, the account executive at Jeppsen's ad agency.

I called out, "Hi, Laurie! Hello, Steve!"

They both glanced up suddenly, looking somewhat startled, almost as if they'd been found with their fingers in the cookie jar. They waved briefly, then immediately got back to their hand-holding. I don't think they saw us wave back.

Moments later, seated at our table, Lisa raised her wine goblet. "Here's to us, Johnny!"

I clinked my glass against hers. "I'll drink to that!" I said. "And I'm glad Laurie has found someone, too. Steve's a good guy."

"Yes, he is. But I like who I found better."

During dinner we both made an effort to avoid talking about the near-tragic occurrence of the afternoon. Nor did we want to discuss Bart Jeppsen's murder or any of the other bizarre and macabre events of the past ten days. Instead, we chatted about the successful sales meeting and the glorious weekend we'd enjoyed at Lakeway. But still, in the back of my mind, sober thoughts were churning, tumbling and running into each other wildly like clothes in a washing machine.

Again that night, lying in Lisa's arms, fitful dreams kept crossing my vision. They popped into view, rapidly and incoherently—seemingly unconnected with each other—switching on and off like various channels on TV. None of it made any sense whatsoever.

But still, throughout the long night, something in my subconscious kept insisting that it all *did* make sense. Somehow, it *must* fit together. Bart Jeppsen's murder, Sid Markowitz's tongue, the bombing of my car outside the Wahoo Lounge, our terrifying approach into Hobby Airport that afternoon, Marty Angel's illegal empire—surely they were not just coincidences.

The pieces were all there, I knew. They just wouldn't fit together.

Finally, toward morning—I had no idea of the exact time—I fell into a deep untroubled sleep. The puzzle was still unsolved, I didn't care.

But then, as things occasionally happen, I suddenly woke up. At last, like a flash of lightning, it came to me. I'll never know how, but I knew the answer.

I leaped up and switched on a lamp. The clock on the night table read 5:45. "Lisa!" I yelled. "I've got it!"

She stirred and rolled over sleepily. "Got what?"

"The whole thing! The solution we've been looking for!"

She stared at me, wide awake now. "You mean you know who killed Bart?"

"Yes, dammit! I know who—and I know why. Jesus! Talk about not seeing the forest for the trees!"

"For God's sake, Johnny, stop talking in riddles! Tell me!"

But then I began to realize that I didn't really *know*. Not through any solid, tangible evidence, certainly not with anything that could be proved in a court of law. All I had was a hunch, a weird, crazy idea. But, in my own mind, I felt sure I was right.

"Lisa, darling," I said, "it's just too tenuous to tell even you. Yes, I think I know the answer—no, I'm *certain* I know—but there's only one way to prove it. And, as it happens, I'm the only person who can find that way. All it'll take is one more trip to the rig. I'm sorry, honey. You'll just have to wait a little while longer."

"Well, hell," she said, getting out of bed. "I certainly won't sleep any more now."

She fixed breakfast, and once more, we headed out to Jeppsen Oil Tool.

33

EVEN AT 7:30 A.M., the scene in Roger Lathrop's office looked almost like a New Year's Eve Party. Roger, Charlie Delman and Dan Trimble had all arrived early, and they were now toasting each other with their coffee cups, celebrating the success of the sales meeting and the future that lay ahead.

"Hey, Johnny," Roger called. "Come join us! You too, Lisa. You should be in on this. You both had a lot to do with it."

It was evident that they'd forgotten all about Bart Jeppsen's murder, for the moment, at least. I hadn't. Now that the final resolution seemed almost within my grasp, it was uppermost in my mind.

"Just a minute, Roger," I said. "I've got to make a phone call first."

I stepped back into the office I still had on loan from Dave Marshall and dialed Grundy Aviation. As I'd hoped, Martha Grundy was also on the job early; people in general aviation work long hours.

"Oh, Mr. McCoy! You caused quite a commotion when you came in yesterday afternoon," she told me over the wire. "The tower has been clamoring for an explanation, and the FAA inspector is due here later this morning. What happened?"

"I'm not really sure, Mrs. Grundy," I said. "But I told the tower I'd prepare a written report. I'll bring it with me next time I come out."

"When will that be? I'm sure it wasn't your fault, but you know the FAA. Sometimes they get pretty sticky."

"Yes, I do know, Mrs. Grundy. But this time it couldn't be helped. Anyway, that's why I called you. I want to make another trip out to the Calco rig. When do you expect Jack in the office?"

"I can't say for certain. He's been down in Corpus Christi again—you probably guessed that—and he usually gets in by noon. But the weather bureau has been announcing some severe weather to the south, with a solid line of thunderstorms and hail, so he may be delayed. I've always told him not to take chances. God, if anything happened to Jack, I don't know what we'd do."

"I understand, Mrs. Grundy. Just call me, please, if you hear anything more. It's important. As I said, I want to schedule another flight to the rig as soon as possible."

"Of course, Mr. McCoy. I'll keep you posted."

I thanked her, depressed the key and immediately dialed the Flight Service Station. The local weather appeared to have cleared, but as Mrs. Grundy had said, that didn't mean it was clear a hundred or more miles away.

I waited impatiently through six rings. Finally my call was answered. "Houston Flight Service Station."

"This is Bonanza 3682-Lima," I said. "I just want to find out. . . ."

The controller interrupted sharply. "3682-Lima!

Are you the guy who almost hit the Exxon Building yesterday?''

"Yes, but . . . ."

"God, that's all I've been hearing since I came on duty this morning. Glad you got down in one piece."

"Me, too," I assured him. "But, look, I need some weather information."

"Where are you going this time?"

"I'm not," I said patiently. "I'm waiting for someone. He's coming in from . . . ."

"It doesn't make much difference *where* he's coming from," the controller interrupted again. "The weather map looks almost like a doughnut. Houston is wide open, but there's a ring of heavy stuff extending in all directions around us. So if your friend is flying a light aircraft—and if he's got any sense—he won't try to get here anytime soon."

"When do you figure the stuff will start breaking up?"

"Probably tomorrow, maybe late this afternoon. Who knows?"

"Okay, thanks. I'll keep in touch." I hung up.

I buzzed Roger Lathrop's office on the intercom. "Hi, Roger. Do you need me right away?"

"Not really, Johnny. We're still just celebrating. But if you've completed your phone call, we'd like you to join us. As I said, you've been a big help around here."

"Thanks. I'll be there in a half hour."

I knew that Martha Grundy hadn't been kidding about the FAA's concern regarding my near miss over downtown Houston. And my communication with the tower hadn't been strictly according to

Hoyle. It wasn't my fault, of course, and I *did* bring the Bonanza down safely, which was obviously the major objective. But, nevertheless, a full report was indeed in order. I spent the next thirty minutes writing it out, narrating the events of the flight, and especially the approach, in complete detail.

I'd just handed it to Lisa for typing, when a now-familiar figure appeared in the doorway. It was Randy Jeppsen.

"Hello, Johnny," he said tentatively. "Can I see you a minute?"

"Sure, Randy. And this time, if you want, we can make it private."

He shook his head. "No, if you don't mind, I'd like Roger Lathrop in on our discussion, too."

"Fine. He's meeting with Charlie Delman and Dan Trimble, the new general sales manager. But they're not all that busy. Why don't we join the group?"

He looked hesitant, even a little scared. Then he straightened his shoulders, and his jaw jutted out somewhat like Bart Jeppsen's in the large portrait that still hung over the foyer entrance below.

"Why not?" he said. "Maybe that'd be best for everyone."

I opened the door to Roger's office, and Randy followed me inside. The hubbub of conversation stopped instantly. Mouths remained open.

"Hello, Randy," Roger said, staring in disbelief. "What brings you here?"

"Just this, Roger. I'd like a job."

"A job! Here? At Jeppsen Oil Tool?"

"That's right. Look, I know I don't have a claim on anything, and I certainly can't expect you or anyone else to give me a cushion or hand me any gravy.'' His eyes swung around the room, then back to Roger. "But I've been doing a lot more thinking. If I can hook up with this company—on whatever basis you say—then maybe I can be of some value down the road. Value to you, and to myself.''

"That's quite a speech, Randy,'' Roger commented. "I don't think I've ever heard you talk like that before.''

"I don't think I've ever heard *myself* talk like that before.'' He looked at me out of the corner of his eye. "Maybe people can change for the better.''

"I've got just one question, Randy,'' I interjected. "Have you decided what you're going to do with the Wahoo Lounge, and how you're going to pay off that $50,000 debt to Marty Angel?'' I didn't want to be unduly hard on the guy—he *did* seem wholly sincere—but I figured it was time to bring everything out in the open.

He leveled his eyes at me. "Yes, Johnny. I've already taken care of that. I sold my interest in the club to Marty Angel in payment for what I owed him.''

"You've got that in writing?'' I asked.

"Sure have.'' He withdrew a folded sheet of paper from his pocket and held it out to me. "Here it is.''

I glanced at it and handed it across the desk to Roger. "I'd say he's a free man.''

Roger read over the document carefully. "This looks all right,'' he said slowly, thumbing his jaw. He took off his glasses and wiped them deliberately with his handkerchief. He replaced them on his

pink face and riveted his eyes on Randy. "But what
could you actually *do* for us? After all, these fel-
lows here—" he waved his hand toward Charlie
Delman and Dan Trimble "—have spent a lifetime
in the oil patch. You haven't."

"Neither has Johnny McCoy," Randy pointed
out. "Yet you seem satisfied with his efforts."

"Yes, but Johnny's a PR man," Roger said. "He's
a professional."

"How long will he be around?"

Roger looked at me and I shrugged. "Not much
longer," I said. "I think my job's almost over."

"Then how about letting me start a PR department within the company?" Randy said. "I've
done some of that sort of thing, you know. Pay me
whatever you want to start, and we'll go from
there."

Roger looked at Charlie and Dan. "You fellas
have any objection?" They shook their heads and I
nodded my own approval. He slapped both palms
on his desk, stood up and extended his hand. "By
golly, Randy, you've got yourself a deal."

This was indeed a bright new day for Jeppsen Oil
Tool—and for the entire Jeppsen family.

But personally, my mind kept going back to the
kaleidoscopic dreams that had troubled me all
night—and to the insane solution with which I'd
awakened early that morning.

I had told Roger that my job was almost over. It
was. But I still needed to make one more trip to the
Calco Oil rig in the Gulf of Mexico. That's where it
all had started. And that was the only way I'd nab
Bart Jeppsen's killer.

34

DURING THE REST of the morning, and throughout most of the afternoon, I made repeated phone calls to the Flight Service Station. The result remained the same.

"Sorry, no change," the controller kept saying wearily. "That solid line of thunderstorms hasn't moved. Only the airlines are coming through, and they're not having an easy time of it."

At last, just before four o'clock, there was finally a word of encouragement. "It looks as if it's beginning to break up," he told me. "It's still no picnic, but a qualified IFR pilot might be able to get through."

"Thanks," I said. "That's all I was waiting for."

I dashed out of the building, jumped into my car and sped toward Hobby Airport. Twenty minutes later, I screeched to a halt outside the Grundy Aviation hangar.

Martha Grundy greeted me as usual. "Oh, hello, Mr. McCoy," she said. "Do you have that report the FAA has been asking for?"

"Sure," I said. "Here." I tossed it to her across the counter. "But never mind that now. Has Jack landed yet?"

"No, but he's on his way. He phoned a couple of

hours ago. I'm sorry I forgot to call you right away.
I remembered later, but Lisa Wallace said you'd
already left. Anyway, the weather's clearing to
the south. As soon as he gets in, I'm sure he'll be
able to fly you out to the rig."

"That's fine, Mrs. Grundy," I said. "I'll be glad
to wait."

After all I'd been through for almost two
weeks, it wasn't easy to just sit there. I kept
trying to make small talk with Martha Grundy,
but conversation was difficult. Mainly, I lit ciga-
rettes, while she continued to heave her heavy
bosom.

Finally, almost an hour later, the Skylane landed
on runway thirteen and taxied up to the parking
area. I was there to greet it.

"Hello, Jack," I called as he got out of the airplane. "I need to make another fast trip to that
rig. Can you take me out right away?"

"Hi, Johnny," he said, walking toward me, his
curly red hair blowing in the breeze. He looked at
his watch. "It's getting pretty late. What say we
do it tomorrow?"

"Sorry. It's important for me to get out there today. I hope you don't mind."

He shrugged. "Okay, if you say so. Let me just
leave my bag in the office."

He deposited his fold-up garment bag in the
Grundy lounge, then walked me back to the red-
and-white helicopter parked on the ramp. He was
still lugging his black vinyl map case, the kind you
always see carried by airline pilots. He placed it on
the back seat and motioned me around to the
other side.

"Might as well ride up front his time," he said. "I hate feeling like a chauffeur."

"Sure, be glad to." I climbed into the left seat. "Why do helicopter pilots fly from the right," I asked, "when airplanes and cars are always driven from the left?"

He shrugged. "Damned if I know. That's just the way it is, I guess. What do you expect to find at the rig this time, Johnny?"

"We'll just have to see," I said.

Once more, he expertly fed power to the rotor blades, and the Bell helicopter lifted gently into the sky. Dusk was just beginning to settle over the Texas coastline as we passed over Galveston.

I waited until we were over the blank void that was the Gulf of Mexico. Then I casually remarked, I'll bet you didn't load a bomb on *this* chopper, Jack."

He looked startled, then laughed. "What the hell do you mean by that, Johnny? Quit kidding, will you?"

"I'm not kidding, Jack. *You* killed Bart Jeppsen, didn't you?" I reached into the back seat and quickly opened the black vinyl map case. There, as I'd suspected, were the ledgers of Marty Angel's criminal empire—the evidence Sid Markowitz had been killed for. "You didn't come from Corpus Christi today. You flew in from Chicago."

Jack Hamilton took his feet off the rudder pedals and grabbed the stick with his knees. Still operating the collective with his left hand, he reached into his pocket with his right and brought out a .22 revolver. He trained it on me and said, "Okay, you bastard. You think you've got it all figured out. But after I drop your dead body into the Gulf, it won't do you much good. So tell me, Mr. Smart-ass, how did you come to this brilliant conclusion?''

"It started with all your busman's holidays. Martha Grundy said you were always in Corpus Christi, but I began to wonder, especially with those Mexican charts in the file cabinet.''

"Go on,'' he snarled. "This is getting interesting.''

"Okay,'' I said. "Glad to oblige. When Marty Angel got that phone call Thursday night at the Wahoo Lounge, I figured it must have been connected with the evidence that had been given to Sid Markowitz. He told somebody to bring it to him. That somebody was you.''

Jack Hamilton still had his revolver pointed directly at my chest. The helicopter was holding a steady course over the Gulf of Mexico, the rotors whining their rhythm overhead.

"What's all that got to do with Bart Jeppsen?'' he asked. His red freckles were now ugly splotches.

"Nothing. That's the sad part. And that's what put us all off the track. You were damned clever, Jack.''

He bowed slightly, without letting the revolver waver an inch.

"But not quite clever enough,'' I went on. "Everybody assumed that the bomb had been loaded aboard that chopper at the rig. Nobody guessed it had been put in place *before* the chopper even left the airport, that it was set to explode only after the *second* takeoff. But that's the way you must have rigged the ADF on my Bonanza, too, and that's how I got that false reading during my approach yesterday into Hobby, the approach that nearly took us into the Exxon Building.''

"Brilliant!'' Now that he had me helpless, he seemed to be thoroughly enjoying himself. "But I still say, what's that got to do with Bart Jeppsen?''

"And I still say, nothing. He was only an innocent victim, just the way Lisa Wallace would have been yesterday afternoon. But you didn't care, did you, Jack? As I say, it was damned clever. Everybody was looking for someone with a motive to kill Bart. Nobody thought anyone had a reason to murder Herb Grundy. But you did. You were working with Marty Angel, smuggling dope up from Mexico. Herb must have found out. He probably threatened to turn you in. That's why you killed him.''

Finally, Jack Hamilton gave full vent to his emotions. "Damn right! Do you think I wanted to spend the rest of my life working for that chicken-shit outfit? Herb had me doing everything from pumping gas to washing airplanes. And he paid me eight bucks an hour. Big deal! Marty Angel showed me some real dough, and I grabbed it. Why not?'' His eyes narrowed. "Who else knows about this, McCoy?''

"Nobody,'' I said. "I wasn't sure, myself. That's why I wanted to take this little ride with you today.''

"So this was all a big bluff, huh?''

"Sort of. What really started me thinking was the article in *Flying Magazine* that I read in your office the other day.''

"What article?'' It was crazy, but he sincerely wanted to know.

"It was called 'The Ocean-Hoppers.' One of the sections was about Wiley Post."

"So?"

"It told how Wiley Post was killed in Alaska back in 1935. His passenger was the great Will Rogers. And the newspapers concentrated all their attention on *him*, just the way they did with Bart Jeppsen. I didn't realize it at the time, but *that's* what actually tipped me off."

"You smart sonofabitch! Get ready to die!"

Jack Hamilton then brought the revolver across his body, ready to fire point-blank at my chest. At that short distance, there was no way he could miss. And I knew he wouldn't hesitate any longer. He'd simply squeeze the trigger and then throw my corpse out the door, into the vast Gulf of Mexico. I had only one slender chance. I took it.

Used for training as well as charter, the Grundy Aviation helicopter had dual controls. I slammed my right foot on the rudder pedal. Hard. The chopper spun to the right, almost like a top. The sudden centrifugal force threw Jack against me, bringing the revolver around ninety degrees. As he fired, the bullet creased my sleeve and buried itself in the back of the seat. I gave a sharp karate chop to the side of his wrist, and with a howl, he let the gun slip from his fingers. It clattered onto the floor.

We scuffled for a few minutes, as the helicopter careened wildly through the sky. Hamilton was not a large man, but he was quick. And we both were desperate. It was clearly a fight to the finish.

Finally, the revolver slid directly between us. As Jack reached down to pick it up off the floor, I slammed my heel onto his open fingers, then instantly brought the edge of my open hand sharply against his Adam's apple. He let out a yelp of pain and slumped over. He was out cold.

Turning toward the north, I spoke into the mike.

Back at Hobby Airport, we were greeted by Lieutenant Mendez and several uniformed members of the Houston Police Department. Jack Hamilton was just coming back to life.

As the cops clamped handcuffs on his wrists, he said, "You sonofabitch! I thought you told me you didn't like helicopters."

"That's right," I said. "But I didn't tell you I couldn't fly them."

Lieutenant Mendez then turned his attention to the map case. With eyes gleaming, he scanned the evidence that would now convict both Hamilton and Marty Angel.

Fingering his mustache, he said, "We have a saying in Spanish for this, too, McCoy: *gracias*."

Be a detective.
See if you can solve the...

Raven House
MINUTE MYSTERY

On the following page is Raven House
MINUTE MYSTERY #1, "A Lie Gets the Ax."

Every month each Raven House book will feature a
MINUTE MYSTERY, a unique little puzzler designed
to let *you* do the sleuthing!

Check your answer by calling (in U.S.A. only)
1-800-528-1404 during the months of August,
September and October 1981. Canadian and U.S.
residents may obtain the solution by writing any time
during or after this period to:

Raven House MINUTE MYSTERY
1440 South Priest Drive
Tempe, AZ 84281
U.S.A.

A LIE GETS THE AX

"The body's under the woodpile, but remember—you gotta keep me outa this," whined Stig Carona, casting shifty eyes at Professor Fordney and Inspector Kelley. Sniffing through a nose that an ungenerous nature had placed at an unlovely angle and licking lips cut on the bias, Stig twisted his greasy cap in nervous fingers.

An hour later the three men got out of a police car and walked to a clump of bushes in Wilson's woods.

"Bill and Jake were fightin' in front of that shack over there," Stig explained, pointing to a clearing. "Jake knocked Bill down, then grabbed an ax. When Bill got up Jake hit him over the head with it a couple of times. Then he dragged the body toward the shack. He must've thought he heard somethin' 'cause he propped it up against the house and walked over this way. I knew if he found me here I'd get what Bill got, so I lammed to the road, jumped in my car and went for the cops."

Fordney observed bloodstains on the shack about three feet from the ground, which appeared to bear out Stig's story. Some freshly cut firewood spattered with dark stains lay near a chopping block.

Opening the door of the shack the professor was about to enter when Kelley called from the yard. "The body's under the woodpile, all right. Gad, what a sight!"

But Fordney's interest at the moment was not the body but a bright, clean, shining ax standing in the far corner of the shack's single room. Carrying it by its battered handle, he took it outside. At the professor's quiet words Stig turned with a startled look.

"Unless," said Fordney, "you want to be placed under arrest for murder immediately, you will tell us the truth about this crime."

How did Fordney know Stig's account was untrue?

From **Minute Mysteries** by Austin Ripley.
Copyright © 1949 by Opera Mundi, Paris.